MOONLIGHT
SONATA

A STORY OF LIFE IN THE SHADOWS

LEONIE PEARCE

First Edition published 2020 by
2QT Limited (Publishing)
Settle, North Yorkshire BD24 9RH United Kingdom
Copyright © Leonie Pearce 2020
The right of Leonie Pearce to be identified as the author
of this work has been asserted by him/her in accordance with the
Copyright, Designs and Patents Act 1988

Cover Design by Charlotte Mouncey with author's own images and drawings
Printed in Great Britain by Ingram Sparks

A CIP catalogue record for this book is available
from the British Library
ISBN 978-1-913071-90-5

This is a work of fiction and any resemblance to any person living or dead
is purely coincidental. The place names mentioned are real but have no
connection with the events in this book

For Isobel and her family

*'It is no measure of health to be adjusted
to a profoundly sick society.'*

Jiddu Krishnamurti

Prelude

Clare: June 12th 1964

In our house you always know when there's going to be a storm, because the seagulls fly inland and settle on the chimney pots. They fight over scraps and make a racket. Dad says they're a flaming nuisance, keeping people awake at all hours. He says they should take a long walk off a short pier.

The house has five floors. From the balcony you can see for miles, over the gardens, over the coast road, over the railings, over the pebbles and out to sea. If you could look over the horizon you would see France. The outside of our house looks like the Darlings' house in *Peter Pan*. It's tall, with iron railings and a basement, painted cream like all the others in Adelaide Crescent. Our family has lodgers and we mustn't make a noise and disturb them.

In the front room on the second floor there used to be a major who had a moth-eaten tiger rug. He set fire to the house and had to go. On the ground floor there's a retired monk who thinks serious thoughts, and a quiet couple called Mr and Mrs Smith. Miss Searle lives down in the basement with two chickens. She eats lots of egg sandwiches and these days she never speaks, though she used to years ago and we called her Auntie Violet. When we were small she helped with the cleaning and sometimes took us children out to the gardens or the beach. Mum says to be kind to her because she lost her only love in the Battle of the Somme. She's supposed to be my godmother but I wish she wasn't. She sends me birthday cards and the other day she waved to me from the basement steps but I pretended not to see. Dad said that last week, when he was bending down to check her electric meter, she tried to comb his hair then sang a hymn. She stares at me like a cross-eyed chicken. It gives me the creeps.

If you're outside and put your hand through the letterbox, you can find a key on a string and unlock the front door. Dad doesn't like the fact that anyone can walk in, but there's nothing worth nicking in the hallway, just a rusty bicycle, some woolly hats and scarves and a bag of muddy golf clubs. There's a hall-stand with a mottled mirror and a pile of old advertising flyers, where Mum puts the post. The air smells of incense, mould, lavender polish and whatever's cooking. The floor's tiled in a black and white pattern and it's always dingy because there's only one light bulb for the hall and the foot of the stairs. The wooden bannister is perfect for sliding down. It feels like flying, but we are not allowed to do it.

The wallpaper's called The Strawberry Thief and you can get lost in the pattern: birds and flowers and leaves, stretching upwards like a forest full of secret whispers and echoes. Sometimes you hear Dad playing the piano upstairs and forget about the world outside. My favourite piece is the *Moonlight Sonata*, but I am not allowed to ask him to play it because it reminds him of growing up without a birth mother or father, and he gets miserable. Mum says we have to shut the door and leave him to it. There are too many closed doors and things we can't talk about in this house.

I love my dad but he has spells when he gets moody. When

he's like it we have to do what Mum calls treading on eggshells. She says the moods are because he had a miserable childhood. He was adopted by an old couple who didn't know much about children. They made him go to mass, morning, noon and night and be an altar boy, which meant he couldn't play football on Sundays with his mates. It put him right off religion and he won't come to services with us, even at Christmas.

In the war, Dad went to sea as a radar operator. While he was in the navy, the old people died and left him this house. He came back to England and married Mum and they had the seven of us, four boys and three girls. I'm Clare. I'm twelve, and the third. I like being third. Three's my lucky number.

The statue of St Anthony lives on the sill of the arched window halfway up to the first floor. Mum backs past it on her hands and knees with a dustpan and brush when she cleans the stairs. Miss Searle used to clean them before she got too old. Mum says she doesn't mind doing them herself these days, because it's her penance and she always has a word with St Anthony on the way down. Sometimes she leaves some incense and a night light in a red glass pot beside him, to thank him for keeping watch over us all.

Once, my sister Susie was sliding down the bannisters and fell with a horrible crash from the first floor onto the tiles below. She lay with her head sideways and one arm stuck out at a strange angle, as if she was trying to do a thumbs-up. She went white as chalk and never made a sound as Dad carried her to the ambulance. The next day she came home with her arm in a sling. Mum said St Anthony had looked after her, because falling all that way she could have died. Girls are not made to fly.

Near where Susie fell there's a glass panel in the floor, to let light into the basement. The glass got damaged one day when the major dropped a cannon ball on it. It cracked into a shape like a spider's web. Dad says it's safe, but I always feel nervous about it giving way under my feet, in case I fall through into the basement, down into the dark and scary world of Miss Searle.

Today something happened that's given me goose bumps. I found a letter on the hallstand, addressed to me. The envelope is a big brown one with what feels like a bundle of papers inside. Outside, in spidery black handwriting, it says:

TO CLARE - IMPORTANT: PLEASE READ CAREFULLY.

I haven't opened it yet. Looking at the writing I'm pretty sure I know who it's from. Am I imagining things? Why would Miss Searle write to me? It's not my birthday. I've got a funny feeling like something is about to change; like a storm is on the way.

The Basement Flat,
4, Adelaide Crescent,
Hove

11th June 1964

Dear Clare,

You are probably surprised that I am writing to you, because it's not your birthday. You may think I'm losing my marbles, but please read on. You'll be amazed at how much we have in common .

Sometimes I see you walk past my window on your way to school and I think you look a bit like me when I was young. You have the same straw-coloured hair and often you seem to be in a daydream, like I used to be. You have a kind face. I am hoping you will read my story and pass it on to your mother and father. They are more likely to listen to you than to read something from me.

By the time you read this I shall have gone away. Your parents no longer want me here. I have found another place where I will be happy.

I have been writing my story ever since I took a vow of silence, several years ago. It tells how I discovered my gift and learned to use it, how I lost my dearest love, how I survived dark days and made good and how I was cast down by doing wrong to please others, before I learned to

11

be strong in my own ways.

As you know, my first name is Violet. I am named after a flower that stands for modesty and wisdom, though I haven't always been modest or wise. My surname is Searle, which is like the French for 'alone.' I am happy being alone because I can be free to think my own thoughts and be in my own world.

My life has been a journey up the steep slopes of Make Sense Mountain. I have travelled rough tracks over the Hills of Hard Work and learned to fly through valleys of Dark Days to the shingly place of the Whispering Waves. Here is a secret. I have collected some magic water from the Whispering Waves at midnight, when the tide was low and the light of the moon sparkled on the sea. I keep it in a bottle to remind me of my days as Wendy Moon.

A few days ago your father brought a doctor to see me, because he thinks my mind is wandering and I need to be looked after in an institution. I said I would give the doctor some of my writing to look at. He said he would call again next week to see how I was getting on. Good luck to him. I shall have moved by the time he comes back. I want you to know my story, so I'm giving you my writing.

I have made mistakes in life but I am not a bad person. I like to think that one day we may get to know each other better.

Bless you and your family, my dear.

With love,

Violet

MY STORY
BY VIOLET SEARLE

FLYING

1905

I was born near Worthing, on the south coast, and lived with my parents at their market garden.

When I was five I saw the play of *Peter Pan*. It changed my life. From then on I knew there were more wonders in the world than I'd ever dreamed of. I believed in fairies and wanted to fly like Wendy Darling.

Watching *Peter Pan* I left behind my everyday life. The muddy lane to Brandy Land, the endless rows of tomatoes in glasshouses and the sap that stained your fingers just disappeared like water down a drain. The Theatre Royal opened up a world of magical lights, strange noises, flashing swords, pretty mermaids, wicked pirates, a real fairy, a ticking crocodile and children who could fly. When you found that place you could be what you wanted.

Peter had sparkly eyes, emerald green tights, silver boot buckles and a jacket as red and shiny as a ladybird's wings. Wendy was a kind girl who helped Lost Boys and sewed Peter's shadow back on, so he taught her to fly. I would have done the same thing in her place. I was desperate to learn to fly. On the way home I asked Mother about flying and she explained that the people in the play were really actors who used special harnesses attached to ropes to lift them up. You couldn't fly in real life and I was not to try. Some children in London had seen the play and tried jumping off high-up things and they got badly hurt.

After our trip to the play I started having dreams about flying. In the dreams I had special powers. I would stand still and concentrate, then push the air down hard on either side of me with the palms of my hands till I floated straight upwards and hovered. Other people were impressed by the flying, especially when I tilted onto my side and steered around the room and out of the window. Now and then a few would be jealous but it didn't stop me. Flying felt so good I wanted to go on doing it for ever.

When we got back home after the play life seemed so dull. Everything I did was ordinary, like cleaning or picking tomatoes or sweeping the floor. The parlour clock ticked and chimed the hours away. School wasn't much better. We had to sit still for hours while Miss droned on and on. I wished our family could be adventurous like the Darlings and find a way through to a magical world. I vowed to myself that when I grew up I'd live in a place like the Darlings' house.

Service

1914

Olive, my older sister, was the clever one. She got on well with Mother and stayed at home to help with the accounts. Frank, my older brother, worked on the market garden with Father, while Mother kept house. I was the odd one out, not needed, there by accident. Father called me Lizzie Dripping. He said I lived in a dream world and if I didn't wake up soon, I'd come to no good.

As soon as I was fourteen and had finished school they got rid of me. I went away into service at the vicarage in Sompting, the next parish, to learn to stand on my own feet. Mother had grown up near there and knew Mrs White, the vicar's housekeeper. The last maid had just left 'under a cloud', and so there was a place to fill straight away. Mother said I was lucky to have such an opportunity. Mrs White was fair, though she could be a bit stern, perhaps because there had been tragedy in her life. She was childless. Her husband had let her down by moving to Oxford and starting a family with a pastry cook. Then her sister had caused 'a great deal of trouble', running away from home and becoming a Catholic nun.

Being in service was a shock. Out of bed at six every morning to clean out the grates and lay up the breakfast, fetch in the eggs from the henhouse and let out and feed the hens. I didn't mind that because Sally, my favourite, used to look out for me and peck the grain from my hand, ever so gently. She was a Cream Legbar and she clucked and ran over to say hello when she saw me, and laid lovely blue eggs. I was allowed one with toast for my breakfast, after I'd finished clearing the vicar's table.

Then there was a cooked dinner to prepare with Mrs White. Afternoons were for darning and mending, polishing the silver and brass and the copper pans, sweeping and dusting. If there was time I might be allowed to go into the garden for a while to look after the flowers on my special patch. I was allowed a special patch on account of it being 'character building' and the vicar thought that growing up on a market garden might have given me green fingers. This was not true, but it meant I got time outside the house.

On Thursdays Brendan, the delivery boy, came round on his bicycle. He'd been in Frank's class at school and knew most of the same people I did. He passed on bits of news, which helped me keep in touch with home. There were days when I needed cheering up because that vicarage felt grim and godforsaken

CARNIVAL

August 1914

Soon after I started work at the vicarage I began having what Mrs White called 'peculiar turns'. It's hard to say how long they lasted because when they came over me I'd lose track of time. I knew when a turn was starting, because I'd get a taste in my mouth like sour gooseberries on a metal spoon. It would creep up my nose like mist and make my thoughts fuzzy, so I'd forget where I was and what I was supposed to be doing. If someone spoke to me it sounded as if they were making bubble noises under water, while I was floating in Cloud Cuckoo Land and wasn't in my body at all. Sometimes after a turn I'd comfort myself by humming a tune that reminded me of *Peter Pan*.

Mrs White said my peculiar turns were on account of my age, which was fourteen, when girls get breasts and bigger hips and start monthlies. She said some girls of my age outgrew their strength for a while and I'd better make sure I was strong enough to pull my weight at the vicarage. She said weakness ran in some families, but from what she knew of my mother it didn't run in hers. She gave me doses of cod liver oil to build me up, but it was disgusting and made me retch, even when I held my nose like she told me to. I wanted to write and tell Mother about the peculiar turns but Mrs White said it was time I let go of Mother's apron strings and stood on my own two feet. In the end, Mother did find out about the turns. This is how.

On the Monday of August Bank Holiday I was allowed a day off to go to the carnival at Steyne Gardens with my family. There were lots of special attractions, including an electric self-starting car which Hudson's Garage advertised as 'particularly suitable for ladies'. The long walk there in my Sunday best was down a hot and dusty lane. At one point I thought about sitting down for a rest, but I didn't want to get my dress dirty.

Just then, a motorbike came up behind me and its engine puttered to a stop. Bobbing to one side I saw a dusty young man dismount. I'd describe him as posh, a toff. He was wearing knickerbockers and I knew at once who he was. I'd seen him in church with his parents and sister, in one of the family pews. They lived in a big house in Broadwater, near to Brandy Land, where we had our market garden. It had an ornamental pond and glasshouses that had been brought over from the Great Exhibition of 1851. His father, who owned the place, was a doctor and he was the first to think of growing tomatoes in England under glass. The tomatoes were a great success and other people copied the idea and made money, including my father's parents. That's how our family came to own a market garden.

'Good morning, young lady,' said the toff, pushing up his goggles.

'Good morning, sir,' I replied with a curtsey. Mother had taught me to show respect to posh people. You never knew if they might take offence.

He laughed. 'No need to call me sir. You can call me Sandy if you like.'

I wasn't sure how to make polite conversation with the gentry. He had reddish brown hair, which gave me a starting point.

'Thank you, sir. Did they call you Sandy on account of the hair? You must have had a lot of hair as a baby.'

He laughed again. I seemed to have a gift for making him laugh.

'Heavens, no,' he replied. 'They call me Sandy because my name's Alexander. Alexander Cross. Pleased to meet you.'

He held out his hand, which was sticky with sweat. I shook it and bobbed another curtsey.

'And your name is…?'

'Violet, sir. Violet Searle.'

'I'm very pleased to meet you, Violet. Are you on your way to the carnival?'

'Yes I am, sir.'

'I'd offer you a lift on my Triumph but I don't think it would be very comfortable for you, riding a motorcycle in a summer frock.'

'No, it wouldn't, sir. I'm happy to walk, sir.'

'Where do you live, Violet? I'm sure I've seen you before.'

'I grew up with my parents at Searle's Market Garden, sir. But now I'm in service at the vicarage in Sompting.'

'Jolly good show, Violet. I knew I'd seen you around here before. Mind you, I've been up at Balliol for most of this year.'

'Balliol sir? Whereabouts is that?'

'Ah, yes. You may not have heard of it. It's a college in Oxford, where I'm reading History. Bowlby, my old headmaster, put me onto it. Mind you, I'm not sure whether I'll be back there next term.'

'Why not, sir? Don't you like it there?'

'Like it? Goodness me. I like it well enough. No, no. I don't suppose you've heard about all the trouble in the Balkans.'

23

I had no idea what he was talking about.

'The Balkans, sir?'

'Yes, overseas. There's talk of war there soon. I may be needed as an officer.'

'Talk of war?'

'Yes, war. No need to sound like a parrot, Violet.'

'Sorry, sir. War, sir? In England, sir?'

'No, no. Heaven forbid! The war will be fought across the channel. But England could be involved and it will be all hands on deck.'

His words shocked me cold. What about my family? I felt the blood drain from my head. He must have seen me go pale because he took my hand and patted it.

'Now then, there's nothing for you to worry your pretty head about. If there's a war it'll be over by Christmas. Everything at the vicarage will stay just as it always is.'

'But sir, that's terrible news. What about my family?'

'Violet, I want you to do something for me. Whatever happens, you must always be a brave girl and think of England.'

'Yes sir. I'll do my best.' But I didn't feel brave.

'Tell me now! What must you do?'

'Be brave, sir, and think of England.' I could do it. I could fly like Peter Pan if I had to.

'Good girl. Now then, let's think no more about it. Let's be off and enjoy the carnival.'

With those parting words he replaced his goggles and puttered away on his Triumph.

My worries disappeared as soon as I got to the carnival and saw my family. A bite of Mother's home-made gingerbread made me instantly more cheerful. Frank and his friend,

Brendan, treated us all to elderflower cordial from a home-made stall. Father and the boys went off to look at the self-starting car while Mother and I guessed the weight of an enormous cake. My sister Olive wanted to visit Gypsy Rose Lee, who was telling fortunes. Mother thought fortune telling was superstitious and a waste of money but, while she was busy talking to a friend from church, Olive grabbed my arm and dragged me over to the far edge of the lawns where there was a small tent with a painting of a crystal ball.

'Stop it. Let me go!' I cried, afraid she was going to pull me inside with her.

'You're such a baby,' she hissed. 'I've got some proper grown-up questions to ask. Teddy's proposed.'

She pulled something out of her pocket. It was a letter with a heart drawn on the envelope, beside her name. She kissed it and held it against her cheek.

'Watch out for Mother and whistle if she comes, scaredy-cat,' she whispered as she went inside the tent. My heart beat fast and I froze to the spot like a shocked rabbit.

Suddenly I could taste gooseberries and the crystal ball picture went foggy. The brass band sounded like the rumble of an engine. I wanted a good shepherd to guide me through the Valley of Darkness so I could lie down and rest, but instead I found myself hovering over a muddy field, with ear-splitting bangs and rumbles in the distance, coming nearer. There were men crawling face downwards in the mud, carrying guns. Some of them were hurt and crying and there was an evil smelling mist drifting over their heads. I wanted to help but I couldn't move. I could feel grass under my face and sticks and stones poking into my arms and legs, then someone was grabbing me, pushing and prodding all over me and into my body's secret places. Would Mrs White be angry about bruises and stains on my best dress? I tried to sit up but I was being forced down so hard it hurt. I gave up struggling. It went on for several moments and then there was a shout.

The poking and prodding had stopped and I opened my eyes. A boy's face was peering into mine and the look of it seemed to change from kind to angry and back. He was pulling my skirt down over my knees. I sat up. My knickers were round one ankle and between my thighs I could feel dampness and a stabbing pain. The boy looked round and saw Olive come out of the fortune teller's tent. She screamed and he ran away. I knew who he was. He was my brother's friend, Brendan.

After that Mother said I was to come home for the night and be taken care of. She sent Frank on his bicycle to tell Mrs White that I was indisposed and needed a day off. Bliss! To be honest, I didn't feel too bad, just a bit shivery and sore in private places.

Mother filled the tin bath with hot water and told me to have a good scrub all over. There were bloodstains in my pants when I took them off. Mother gave me a disapproving look and took them away to wash. Then she put me to bed with a hot water bottle, even though it was summer, and she made me drink a disgusting herbal brew flavoured with juniper berries and honey. It tasted vile but made me feel warm and soppy. Then she asked me about what had happened and I said I couldn't remember, on account of having one of my peculiar turns. She said what kind of peculiar turns? Why hadn't she heard about them before? She was cross that Mrs White hadn't let her know about them, but not cross enough to have words with her because she wanted me to stay on at the vicarage. Mother didn't find me easy to get on with. She said I got under her feet and thank goodness that at least her other daughter was a capable girl.

I didn't say anything to Mother about Brendan being there, because he was always friendly to me and I didn't want to get him into trouble. Olive knew because she'd seen him run away and she told me off about it. She said not to worry about getting anyone else into trouble, because I was the one that might be in trouble. I didn't know what she meant. She seemed to be talking in riddles.

'Brendan's interfered with you, Violet. Don't you even know that?'

As far as I was concerned she was trying to be a know-all.

'Brendan's my friend,' I protested. 'He wouldn't hurt me.'

'Stupid girl!' she replied. 'All boys are the same – only after one thing.'

I tried to think what that might be. Was it an electric self-starting car?

PERFECT TIME

1914

After the upset at the carnival I became shy and withdrawn. I certainly didn't see myself as having a gift. I didn't know who might have witnessed my awkward moments and was afraid of what people might say. Olive, in particular, took me to task, pointing out that my virtue had been compromised. She called me a complete failure.

'You need to keep your mouth shut,' she advised me. 'If word gets around about you being interfered with, you'll have every boy for miles around trying to take advantage.'

'Word won't get round. I won't talk to anyone at the vicarage about it,' I assured her.

'Just as well,' she went on. 'You need to think of me too. What does it do for my reputation if I've got a sister with dirty knickers?'

'Sorry, Olive,' I said. 'I'll make sure I keep them nice and clean.'

I felt confused because I didn't know exactly what had happened at the carnival and whether it was my fault. Mother was tight-lipped about it. Mrs White never mentioned it, though sometimes, when she thought I wasn't looking, she squinted strangely at me, as if she was choosing a piece of pork for the Sunday roast. I did my best not to be clumsy, to speak politely and to look full of virtue.

It felt especially awkward seeing Brendan again, because I remembered his face looking into mine when I was flat on my back on the grass. But when he next delivered groceries at the vicarage he was as friendly as ever. I wanted to ask him if he'd seen what happened, but the thought of talking about it made my hands go clammy and scarlet flushes crept up my neck. Besides, Olive had told me to keep my mouth shut, and she knew best, because she was now, in her own words, 'a woman experienced in matters of the world'.

Meanwhile I was stuck at the vicarage, and Brendan was the only person of my own age I could talk to. The sound of his bicycle bell at the gate made my heart leap with joy. My life was lonely and sometimes I felt as if he was my only friend.

Brendan was the middle one of the five Collins boys. His family were our neighbours in Brandy Land. The place was called Brandy Land because in the old days you could buy an acre of land there for five gallons of brandy, so our grandparents did well to take advantage while it was cheap. Once the tomato growing started the place was smartened up, with proper lanes and fences and bungalows and glasshouses in rows. Children were brought up to be neat and polite and not to throw stones.

Brendan was a third child, like me, but he had two younger brothers, which made him a middle one, like Frank. When they were at school, he and Frank played together, and being two years younger I used to get my plaits pulled, but they sometimes let me into their den in the field at The Plot. The Plot was Brendan's family's place, next to our market garden. His grandparents had come over from County Cork during the Great Hunger when the Irish potatoes got blight and people starved. They got a couple of acres for next to nothing and built a wooden house, a tool shed and a stable for a pony. Brendan's dad grew up there and learned how to repair machines. His brother Mickey got a fishing boat and sold live mackerel for sixpence a bucket, taking it round the bungalows on Shoreham Beach with the pony and cart.

A few years ago Mr Collins got knocked off a bicycle and it made him a bit slow, but he still did repairs, grew potatoes, kept chickens and goats and delivered groceries round the houses. The boys all helped out. Sometimes they took Patches, the pony, down to Shoreham Beach and hauled cartloads of stone. There was a special kind of flint down there that was perfect to grind up and make glass.

Brendan had blue eyes, black curly hair, and freckles on his skin, which was as pale as milk. He could play any tune on the penny whistle. Since I told him about falling in love with *Peter Pan* he started calling me 'Wendy'. In return I called him 'Curly', after one of the Lost Boys. He was the kindest person I've ever known.

Some people called the Collins family tinkers, which they weren't. They were just Irish and went to the Catholic Church. Curly's dad used to make and mend things in his wooden shed. Their field was full of old carts and bits of machinery. The chickens used to roost on them, and Patches, the pony, liked scratching his sides against the metal, which meant he sometimes had engine oil as well as mud on his white bits. Curly had to clean him off with soapy water to get him ready to do the delivery rounds.

Sometimes the boys would take Patches down to the beach and get a cart load of seaweed to spread on their vegetable beds. People laughed at them and said they were backward, but the

Collins family grew the biggest onions and spuds I've ever seen. Curly said that one day he would take me to Shoreham Beach to fetch some seaweed and see his Uncle Mickey's fishing boat.

Curly's mum made tasty biscuits and if I went round with a windfall apple for Patches she would sometimes give me one. She told us stories too, sitting round the wood fire. There was a long and complicated one about a moonstone that got stolen. In another, a goblin king had a baby daughter, and he asked the midwife to put magic potion on the baby's eyes so she could see things that humans couldn't see. When the king wasn't looking, the midwife put some of the potion on her own eye and from then on she could see fairies and goblins up to all sorts. I found an old brandy bottle buried in the garden and tried making magic ointment with rose petals and strawberry leaves, shaken up with rain water. For several nights I dabbed it on my eyelids, then the petals went brown and smelled evil, so I threw it out on the garden. It may have partly worked, because I do see things other people don't.

I never thought much about Curly till I was in service at the vicarage, and seeing him reminded me of home so I felt less lonely. As well as news he would bring me things he found in the fields and hedgerows, like blossom or berries or a polished conker or an ash key from his favourite tree. On my afternoon off we sometimes went for a walk together. He promised me that we would visit his uncle at Shoreham Beach. He planned to live there one day and build a houseboat, where you could sit and watch the sun sparkle on the sea. I was excited, but the war started and the army put barbed wire all along the sea front.

Things changed in the war. The Boy Scouts were trained to help coastguards guard the channel against the enemy. We weren't allowed to light fires at night. We had to be careful what we said and watch out for spies. Curly's older brothers joined the Southdown Battalion, but Curly was still sixteen and stayed at home.

At first we thought the fighting would be over by Christmas, but it dragged on. Goring Hall was turned into a hospital for wounded soldiers. Men disappeared like Lost Boys. Strong-looking horses were taken from nearby farms to pull heavy guns to the battlefields. Curly was worried that Patches might be taken, so he kept him looking scruffy and taught him to lay back his ears and bare his teeth at strangers. Patches was rejected for military service.

In 1916, they brought in conscription and Curly had to sign up, like his older brothers before him. Frank was the same age but got let off because he was growing food for England. Curly told me not to worry about him, because he would look after the horses on the battlefield and find his brothers, then they would all come home safe to their mum and dad. And he would take Molly, his pet mouse, in his pocket for company.

Before he left we had a last walk together across the common land called the Egg Field to the old ash tree. It was spring and the leaves were bursting open from tender green buds.

'I'll think of you while I'm away,' he said, handing me something wrapped in a clean white hankie and looking a bit shy. 'I made this for you to remember me by. Open it and see.'

Inside the hankie he had wrapped a little carving of a flying angel, made from pale wood, with open wings in the shape of ash keys. Her hair was like mine, long and wavy, tied back from her face. She was warm in my hand. It must have taken ages to get her so perfect.

'Thank you,' I said. 'She's like Wendy.'

'Yes,' he replied. 'She's like you too, because you go flying in your dreams.'

I could hardly speak. No one had ever made me something so lovely.

'While I'm away,' he said, blushing a little around his neck, 'may I think of you as my girl? When it's cold and dark and I'm missing home, I'd like to think of coming back here to you, and of us being together properly in a place of our own.'

I didn't know what to say, so I just leaned towards him and kissed him on the mouth. I kissed his dear pale freckly cheeks and wiped tears from his eyes, which were as blue as the willow pattern on my mother's best china. Then I ran my fingers through his curly black hair and stroked him behind the ears, like I'd seen him stroke Patches.

'I'll wait for you,' I said. 'Until you come home you will be Curly, my Lost Boy, and I will fly beside you in your dreams like Wendy.'

He looked at me and smiled and tears ran down his face. He looked so kind and loving. To tell the truth, I felt quite abandoned in a good way, without any awkwardness.

'Do you remember the carnival,' I asked him, 'when I was lying on the grass?'

He looked me in the eye. 'It wasn't me that took advantage. I've never done that … with anyone.' He blushed.

'I didn't think it was you,' I said, suddenly feeling strong and gentle and excited and full of tenderness. 'The carnival was a horrible time,' I said. 'This is a perfect time, here and now.'

The Vicarage
Sompting
West Sussex

25th July 1916

Dearest Curly,

I miss you so much. Last night I walked down across the Egg Field to the old ash tree where we kissed and cuddled and you asked me to marry you. It makes me so proud to be your girl and to think of us setting up home together when the war is over.

Every day I imagine you over in France. Have you still got little Molly Mouse? I wish I could live in your pocket and share your bread like her.

I keep the lovely carving you gave me under my pillow. She is like an angel and I tell her everything. I hide her from Mrs White because she might call me superstitious, talking to a carving. Every night I whisper prayers that she will protect you from the bombs and bring you home safe to England. A few weeks ago in the garden we could hear terrible pounding and thumping coming across the channel, so I can't imagine how loud the battle noises must be for you and poor little Molly Mouse.

Your mum and dad and sisters are well and Patches is getting so fat on summer grass he will hardly fit between the shafts. Your mum is sending you some Woodbines and gingerbread when she can get to the post.

I have a new job, volunteering two days a week as a nursing assistant at the military hospital in Worthing. Can you believe it? It is so sad to see some of the men come in, tired out and confused, and some of them staring blindly from the gas. Do you remember Sandy from the big house? He came to the hospital last week looking very poor and thin. He has forgotten how to wash, shave and get dressed, just stares and mutters to himself. Sometimes he gets violent and has to be strapped down. When I took him his tea and biscuits he called me Mummy and started to cry.

Stay safe, dear Curly. You will always be in my heart.

From your ever loving

Wendy x x x

LOST

Autumn 1916

After Curly got conscripted, we promised to write to one another and stay true. Once he'd been driven away in the army lorry, I woke every morning with a feeling of doom, as though an evil fog had crept in from the sea and I was lost, unable to find my way. People and places that had once been warm and friendly were now cold and distant. I tried to keep my mind on simple everyday things, like cleaning and cooking and volunteering at the military hospital, but all around me things were going wrong.

First, a terrible thing happened to my brother, Frank. He was cutting side shoots off the tomatoes and nicked his finger with a rusty knife. It happened quite often, cutting fingers, but the skin round this cut went puffy and red and a week later he went to bed with a raging fever, a headache and a stiff neck. Mother tried to keep him drinking plenty of water, but his teeth clenched shut and he couldn't swallow properly. She wrapped warm, damp cloths round his neck and jaw, with lavender flowers to relax the muscles, and she rubbed lemon balm on his forehead to take away his headache and help him sleep. The fever did get better, and he perked up and drew a picture of a funny tomato with a cheeky grin and dancing legs. Underneath he wrote 'Be happy!' Then he drifted off to sleep. He never woke up again. In the morning Mother found him, cold and dead as a doornail.

Next I heard the shocking news through Mrs White, news that turned me numb. A few days after Frank had passed away, a telegram had arrived at The Plot to say that Curly and his two older brothers had been killed in action at the Battle of the Somme. It didn't say how they died, but in my mind I could see Curly lying in the mud, his beautiful face bloodstained and bruised, and poor frightened little Molly Mouse squashed to death in his pocket.

I had never felt so alone, with no one to talk to about my sorrow. Mrs White had never really been friendly towards me, so I couldn't confide in her. My parents and Mr and Mrs Collins were lost in their own grief. And my sister Olive no longer had time for me.

She was now married to Teddy Lyons, who drove a van fetching and carrying building materials for the Mystery Towers. The plan was that the two of them would move into our bungalow with Mother and Father, and Teddy would take over from Frank and do the heavy work and deliveries. Olive was expecting a baby at the end of the year and the old bedroom we used to share would make an ideal nursery for the little one.

On top of all the sadness I felt tired and out of sorts. Mrs White told me off for being in a dream and clumsy at my work. It's true that I broke a few cups and saucers. They slipped off the draining board no matter how careful I tried to be.

I put in extra hours volunteering at the military hospital, hoping it would bring me closer to Curly. One of the nurses told me I was looking pale and slipped me extra biscuits with my tea. But I had a funny taste in my mouth, as though I could smell the horrible gas from the trenches that was making our poor boys blind and mad. Food made me feel sick and all I wanted to eat were sour apples off the garden tree. It was a sad time, a time of very dark days.

THE MYSTERY TOWERS

Winter 1916–17

Looking back, those dark days were a confusing time. It is hard to make sense of what happened and when, like opening a box of jigsaw pieces that are from different puzzles so, however hard you try, they will not fit together to make one picture.

One thing that frightened me in the dark days was the Mystery Towers. These were not imaginary. They were part of the war. There were two of them being built by the harbour mouth, overlooking Shoreham Beach where Curly and I had planned to make a home together. We had promised one another to be true, but our plans were spoilt by an evil force.

The purpose of the towers was top secret, though the big one was nearly two hundred feet high, so not very secret. Three thousand men came to camp on Southwick Green and build them. The rumour was they were fortresses to protect us from U-boats but they looked like a gateway of doom. People called them the 'Ugly Sisters' and when the war ended you could pay one shilling and climb to the top for the view. I wrote a poem about them. A kind nurse at the military hospital helped me.

The Mystery Towers   by Violet Searle

Oh great grey towers, you frighten me.
Please keep a watch over the sea,
Defend us from our enemy
And keep our England proud and free!
Please guard the land with all your might
And seek out foes with piercing light.
Don't hide the sky with horrid height
Don't give me bad dreams in the night.
Britons never shall be slaves
They say, but how hard to be brave
With U-boats hidden in the waves
And our boys lost in cold dark graves.
My darling's mouth is filled with earth
Dark blood has stained his brow
And so my days seem nothing worth
Dull grief lives with me now.

BURIAL

Winter 1916

Frank was buried in the churchyard at Sompting, in a grave next to Mother's parents and to Bertie and Louise, her twin brother and sister who had died of diphtheria when they were small. The older children had survived the illness, but the two little ones hadn't had the strength and faded away.

Frank's funeral was a miserable affair. Father was in shock. He was tight-lipped and kept himself to himself. Mother seemed to have aged overnight. Her skin looked yellow and she struggled to stand upright during the service. When the coffin was lowered into the grave she let out a howl, like a fox with its foot caught in a trap. Mrs White held her arm.

A few friends from schooldays, neighbours from Brandy Land and Mother's two remaining brothers, Ernest and Reggie, were at the church. The brothers both worked for the railway company and we rarely saw them. Father was an only child and he decided that the burial would be too upsetting for his parents to attend, so they stayed at home that afternoon.

Some of our friends and neighbours had lost sons in the war. They'd never seen them again after they left for France in their smart soldiers' uniforms. People wept noisily into handkerchiefs at the funeral, thinking of their own lost boys as well as Frank. Everyone sang 'Abide with Me' and the vicar gave a speech, saying that Frank had done his duty for England as much as the boys fighting overseas. I thought of Curly dying all alone in a muddy field far from home, and it seemed to me that Frank had been lucky to pass away in the comfort of his own bed.

Olive did her best to keep everyone in good spirits, which was impossible given the circumstances. She made piles of cucumber sandwiches and got me brewing pot after pot of tea, which I served in the best willow pattern china. Teddy provided nips of medicinal brandy for those stricken with grief. Olive was expecting her first baby soon, and her plump body did seem to offer hope for the future, especially to some of the older ladies.

After the funeral, the days seemed dull and empty, apart from the usual work routine. Curly and Frank were gone. What was there to look forward to? The thought of becoming an auntie should have been a comfort, but there was no longer room for me at home and I felt shut out. My heart was bereft of all I held dear.

My only hope was that if I did my best and worked hard, things might go back to the way they used to be. I cleaned and polished with fervour. The vicar had a butterfly collection, pinned and labelled in glass cases. I kept every one free of fingerprints. Where there is darkness, let there be light. I attended church every Sunday, helping with the flowers, dusting the pews and learning the words of hymns. 'Abide with Me' was a favourite because it reminded me of Frank and Curly and all the lost boys. I spoke the prayers earnestly, even the ones you chant from a book, which I secretly thought were mumbo-jumbo. Every night, before I went to sleep, I lit a candle in front of the angel Wendy and prayed fervently that I would see Curly again. I prayed that there had been a mistake and that he was not dead but hiding at a farm in France, waiting till it was safe to come home. One day I would hear the ring of his bicycle bell and he would be at the vicarage gate, waiting to take me in his arms and kiss me.

I thanked God for understanding that my ways of praying were different from the vicar's. God understood perfectly. One night, holding my little carving of Wendy reminded me how to fly out of my body. I flew to the Egg Field and found a skeleton key from the old ash tree. With this magic key I could unlock the door into a world on the other side. Each time I went there it looked different, but I always found Curly and we talked to each other. My love for him was so strong that he felt like a part of me, the warm and tender part that guided me and kept me alive.

AT THE HOSPITAL

December 1916

At the beginning of December, Olive gave birth to a little girl. The baby was born in hospital so as to have what Teddy's father called 'the finest modern medical care'.

'Nothing but the best for Teddy and Olive,' said Mr Lyons.

In hospital something called 'twilight sleep' was all the fashion for having babies. It sounded peaceful. The mothers-to-be were given morphine and a drug made from nightshade, which stopped them remembering anything. Then they were strapped down in padded cots so they didn't hurt themselves when they thrashed about.

Once the baby was born, Olive stayed in hospital for a week, to rest and to make sure that little Pearl was taking her bottle feeds on the dot. The doctor had told all the new mothers that *Nestles* formula was best for healthy babies.

'That's right. Get them into regular habits from the start,' said Mrs Lyons. She and Mr Lyons were visiting the hospital on the same afternoon as me.

Mr Lyons kept poking a finger at Pearl's nose and saying, 'That's not a nose. It's a button!' in a jolly way, as if he expected us all to giggle at his joke.

Pearl had a snub nose, sea-coloured eyes and a bald head. Her mouth opened and shut like a fish looking for food. She stared intently at Mr Lyons's finger, as though it might be a tasty morsel. For her sake I hoped she would soon grow out of the fish-faced stage.

'She reminds me of you as a baby, Violet,' said Olive.

I wasn't sure whether to be flattered. I had only seen one picture of me as a baby, perched on Mother's knee in a lacy christening dress, with the rest of the family standing proudly round us. Everyone was looking their best for the photograph, but I must have been wriggling because my face was a blur. If I really had looked as peculiar as poor Pearl, it was just as well you couldn't see me properly.

When the baby had been wheeled back to the nursery and Mr and Mrs Lyons had gone, I gave Olive some cakes I'd baked at the vicarage, in a box tied up with pink ribbon. They were made with sultanas, her favourites. She put them to one side.

'I'm on a special diet now,' she said, 'to build up my strength after having the baby.'

'The sultanas might be good for you,' I suggested.

'Don't lecture me!' she said. 'You sound just like Mother.'

I decided to change the subject. 'Did it hurt, pushing out the baby?' I asked.

Olive looked smug, in her older sister way, as if she knew it all and I knew nothing.

'It's a pain like no other,' she said. 'But I don't remember much about it. You can get all the latest drugs here – morphine and so on. I had several injections to bring on the twilight sleep and Pearl was delivered by forceps.'

I had no idea what forceps were.

'Were there really four of them?' I asked, trying to sound impressed.

A nurse came round to take Olive's temperature and to tell

me that visiting time was over, as all the patients were about to be given a cooked meal. I wished Olive would offer me a cake if she didn't want them herself, as I'd walked miles to the hospital and now had to walk back. It was teatime but there was no prospect of anything to eat till I got back to the vicarage. My appetite had improved since Frank's funeral and I felt quite peckish.

I said goodbye to Olive and made my way along hospital corridors, following the Way Out signs. I must have taken a wrong turning, because the place looked unfamiliar. I felt lost and so dizzy I had to sit down in a hurry beside a pile of sheets. Suddenly the world turned upside down and I floated out of my body. There were voices – a woman calling, then a man answering – and I seemed to glide along in a soft mist through dimly lit places, sometimes warm, sometimes cooler. I came to rest leaning against a mossy bank, and felt fingers on my eyes, then something cold against my middle. For some reason I had a kind of dream about the midwife putting ointment on the goblin baby's eyes in the story Curly's mother had told me. Someone must be putting ointment on my eyes too, I thought, and I'd see goblins in the shadows when I woke up.

When I came back into my body I found myself lying on a bed in a small room in the hospital, propped up on pillows. A doctor was nearby, writing on a chart. He had his back to me. A nurse was beside him, cleaning a sort of ear trumpet.

He turned round. 'Ahem! Good. Our patient is awake.' He was wearing tortoiseshell- rimmed spectacles and looked like a startled owl.

I sat up, only to fall dizzily back against the pillows.

'Excuse me,' I said. 'There must have been a mistake. I'm not your patient.'

'Steady on, you've had a nasty turn,' he said. 'I expect you still feel faint. Ahem! It's common in your condition.'

'What condition?' I replied. 'I'm not in a condition.'

'Dear girl,' he said, 'when you're expecting a baby it's normal to feel faint at times.'

'You've got it wrong,' I explained. 'I'm only here to visit my sister, Olive. She's just had a little girl.'

He looked at me thoughtfully.

'Ahem! You'd better stay sitting down for a moment,' he said, taking off his spectacles and wiping them. 'Now, you may not have realised that you are carrying, ahem, a baby. I would estimate the due date is in March. Everything seems to be fine and there's a strong heartbeat.'

I felt a kick inside me and the world turned upside down.

THE ASH TREE

1916

The shock that I was having a baby knocked me completely off balance. It was as if a bomb had exploded, throwing me into the air. My body, drained and useless, lay on the metal bed in the hospital. It seemed best to leave it with the doctor while I made a quick escape, thanks to my gift for flying.

I didn't stay in the hospital. I pressed down hard and kept going, out of a window, over the roof, across a road towards a bushy hill where sheep were grazing, then along a river valley towards the sea. I could see barbed wire along the beach, protecting us from the enemy, and the horrid grey shapes of the Mystery Towers, with men crawling around them like ants. There was the harbour where Curly's uncle kept his fishing boat, a shingle bank with rows of wooden bungalows, a huge glasshouse, a church, and a fort where guns pointed out to sea. For a few moments I felt strangely peaceful, as though this place was home. The vicarage seemed far away. I never wanted to go back and be bossed around by Mrs White, or have to clean the cases of those poor pinned down butterflies.

A chilly wind was starting to whip up white horses among the waves and I made my way slowly inland, flying lower over tufty grass and muddy tracks towards the Egg Field, till I found the old ash tree where Curly and I had promised to be true. Back in summer, the grass had been long and mixed with Oxeye daisies. Curly had made me a necklace, binding their stems and flowers together. Now the daisies were all underground and the soil was littered with the skeletons of dead leaves and ash keys.

'Curly, I miss you,' I whispered, as I circled around the bare winter branches.

'Don't be sad,' he answered. 'I'm watching you.'

His voice sounded clear but I couldn't work out where it was coming from. Was it just in my head?

'Where are you?' I asked.

'You can't see me,' he said, 'but I'm here with you. We can talk to one another.'

It was wonderful to hear him speak, so softly and full of confidence. I flew down to earth and settled under the tree, wishing I could hold him close and look into his willow pattern blue eyes.

'Couldn't I see you as well as hear you, Curly?' I asked, though I was half dreading how he might look.

'Just imagine me beside you, how you remember me,' he answered. 'It's better that way.'

I didn't want to spoil the moment by asking questions about the trenches and the mud and the rats and the corpses of the Lost Boys. It would be much happier to share my new secret, the secret of our baby. Suddenly I was overwhelmed with sadness for us both, and for our baby whose father would never be there for a cuddle.

'It's so lonely without you,' I said, hardly able to keep my voice steady. 'I have something to tell you...' but I couldn't breathe properly to get the words out.

'My lovely girl,' he said. 'I can see everything that's happened

49

to you. You won't always be on your own. Our little one will keep you company.'

The idea of having a little one terrified me, and I snapped straight back at him.

'That's all well and good, but how am I supposed to look after a baby? I can hardly look after myself.'

Curly went quiet for a moment and I knew he was thinking of a plan.

'I'm sorry it's not the way we hoped it would be and I know it's hard for you,' he said. 'But have faith. Everything will come right, I promise. We love each other and we're giving life to a little one. It's a miracle.'

'Yes, it is.' I understood about the miracle. I just didn't have a clue about the practical side of things.

He seemed to know what I was thinking.

'You must tell Mrs White,' he said. 'She'll help you.'

'Oh, Curly,' I replied. 'Mrs White's never had a baby. I can't ask her to help me.'

'Mrs White knows a place where you can go to have the baby,' he said. 'It's an orphanage run by nuns. And if you need help to bring up the little one, the nuns will find people to do it for you.'

'Mrs White? How does she know the nuns? She isn't a Catholic.'

'Her sister's a nun at the orphanage. Don't you remember telling me how upset the family was when she took holy orders? And you found out about the maid who left the vicarage under a cloud. Mrs White helped her by writing to her sister.'

Curly was right. So much had happened lately that my memory was like a sieve. But I needed to be brave, for the baby's sake, and the next day, when I was back at the vicarage, I found the courage to tell Mrs White about my predicament. She was more understanding than I expected.

She went to visit my mother and returned with a letter for me. In it my mother told me that I had always been difficult and headstrong and now, as expected, I had disgraced myself. She and Olive would help me on condition that I stayed well away from the family and kept my shame to myself. It pained her to turn to Catholics for help, but I had left her no choice.

On Mrs White's advice, my mother wrote to Sister Annunciata at The Sisters of the Blessed Virgin Orphanage and Convent and made a donation towards their work. The nuns offered me a bed in one of the dormitories, in exchange for 'domestic duties'. Before it was obvious that I was expecting, Teddy and Olive drove me to my new 'position' in Hove and left me at the orphanage with my nightdress and underwear in a cardboard suitcase, ready to start the next chapter in my life.

CONVENT

1917

The entrance hall of the Sisters of the Blessed Virgin Orphanage and Convent was dark, with a lingering smell of incense and a stone tiled floor, like a church. Scrubbing and polishing that floor was my first job there. Straight in front of the door was a grandfather clock, with a picture of the archangel Michael flying between the sun and the moon, measuring the hours of prayer and labour. Every Tuesday, before vespers, Sister Annunciata wound the clock with a metal key from the bunch she carried on her belt. It had a deep hollow tick and chime that sounded out the hours inside the convent gates. It was easy for the archangel Michael. No one asked him to crawl around and scrub the tiles, weighed down by a baby. He didn't feel any kicks against his bladder that made him run to the lavatory.

The nuns told us that working on our hands and knees was pleasing to the Virgin and for our own good. If we suffered, they told us, it was a penance for our sins and we should be grateful for the opportunity to redeem ourselves. I tried not to hate their grey habits as the nuns glided along the corridors, eagle eyed and reeking of mothballs. I tried not to mind the chilblains on my fingers and the exhausting hours of toil, resting only for prayers in the chapel and meals of mutton and barley broth served with bread and dripping. Food at the vicarage had been luxurious in comparison. How I missed the fresh eggs and milk, vegetables from the kitchen garden and Mrs White's fruit puddings.

The best thing about the convent was finding Anna. Most of the girls in the dormitories looked like I felt. We were pale and quiet, ashamed of the bulges of our unborn babies, too sad for much talk to one another. We walked the corridors in silence, eyes down, sniffing miserably, without words or smiles. Anna was different. I met her one day in the laundry while we were stacking linen. She had dark wavy hair that shone in the pale light from the window and I could see her brown eyes watching me through a gap between the shelves.

'Come and help me fold these sheets,' she called.' It's quicker if we help each other.' Her voice was a bit odd, as if she came from a foreign country.

'Are we allowed to talk?' I whispered.

Anna laughed, as if she didn't care. She held her head up and looked me straight in the eye.

'Who's to know what we do in here?' she said. 'There's only the two of us. Anyway, the nuns can't rule our lives.' She pulled a face, like Sister Annunciata telling us off.

It cheered me up and made me feel brave.

'Where are you from?' I asked.

'I was born in Moscow,' she replied. 'But for the last five years I've lived in Covent Garden.'

I'd heard Father talk about Covent Garden. It was where the tomatoes from our glasshouses were sent on the train.

'Do you sell tomatoes?' I asked.

'Me? Do I look like a tomato seller?'

I wasn't sure whether I'd insulted her, so I quickly replied,

'No, not at all.'

'My name is Anna Tristeva and my mother is a countess,' she said proudly. 'She brought me to England when I was seventeen. We were turned out of our house by the Bolsheviks, before the revolution. My father left us when I was a baby and my mother couldn't manage on her own. She is a hopeless mother, though she did get us both to England to stay with a friend.'

A sharp-eyed nun looked in at the door.

'Quick! Fold this sheet with me,' hissed Anna.

We bowed our heads and tried to look pure in thought, like the statue of the Virgin on the laundry windowsill. The nun glared at us, then glided away down the corridor.

'How terrible for you to be turned out of your home,' I said. 'It happened to me too.'

I'd never met anyone from Moscow before. Anna didn't care about being polite. Perhaps in Moscow everyone said what they thought. I hoped they were on our side in the war. I hoped I could trust her.

'Yes. It was terrible,' said Anna. 'It was much better in Covent Garden. My mother found us work making costumes for the Royal Opera Company. She is good at needlework, but her choice of men is very bad. The last one was my baby's father.'

At first I was shocked by her lack of shame, but gradually I got used to it. In the next few weeks Anna told me more about her life. Her baby girl had been born in January, just before I arrived at the convent. She had called her Nina, but said she probably had another name by now. She had been adopted when she was three weeks old by a wealthy couple from London.

'Don't you miss your baby?' I asked.

'Not really,' replied Anna. 'It's for the best, for her and for me. I can't look after a baby on my own. I need to find work, so I can rent my own place. This convent is driving me mad.'

It was driving me mad too, but where else could I go? I had to put up with it for the sake of my baby. All I could do was nod and sigh.

Anna smiled mysteriously.

'Don't worry,' she said. 'I'm working on a plan for escape. Just wait and see!'

SPRING

1917

The next few months are a muddle in my memory. I remember bits of what happened, but most of it is like a dream that fades quickly when you wake.

Spring arrived. Birds nested in the walled garden at the convent, and it was time for my child to be born. Having Curly's baby safe and warm inside me was comforting, keeping alive our hopes for a life together. I couldn't bear the thought of us being parted.

Sister Eugenie, who looked after the girls when their babies were due to be born, disapproved of the size of my bulge.

'You need to put more effort into scrubbing that floor,' she said crossly. 'It's the way to get things moving. You don't want your baby to be overdue.'

'No, Sister.'

'Look at the size of your bump. The last thing you need is a big baby to push out. They don't just appear one morning under a gooseberry bush, you know.'

'No, Sister.'

'Go and fetch a bucket of warm soapy water and a mop. The back passage needs a good clean.'

'Yes, Sister.'

I was filling the bucket at the stone sink when I noticed warm water dribbling down my leg. At first I thought it must be leaking from the sink and turned off the tap, but the puddle on the tiles grew larger. Nothing like this had happened to me since wetting my pants on my first day at infants' school. The odd thing was that I couldn't feel myself doing it. Relieved that there was no one else around to see my accident, I mopped up the wet patch, cleaned the passage as I'd been told to and then went to change my underwear.

The wetness in my pants was just like water from the tap. Perhaps the sink had overflowed and I was losing my grip on reality, imagining I was an infant again. My back was starting to ache and I felt as though someone had tied string round my insides and was pulling it into tight knots, from several directions at once. I wanted to lie down but I could hear a pitiful wailing and mewing noise, like a kitten having its tail pulled. The poor thing needed to be rescued, I thought, then realised that the sounds were coming out of my own mouth.

The next thing I knew was that Sister Eugenie was holding my arm and insisting I walk with her to the delivery room.

'It's the wrong day,' I was crying. 'Not today, Sister. I'm not ready.'

'You're making too much noise, young lady. No one wants to hear you being so silly.'

I can't remember much that happened after we got to the delivery room. Sister held a funny smelling cloth to my nose and I drifted into uncomfortable dreams and floated out of my body. A doctor arrived and said something about a breech and no time to turn it head first and would someone pass him a scalpel. I was floating near the ceiling, looking down at drops of blood on the floor and hoping I wouldn't get asked to fetch a bucket and mop. I remembered I'd left the soap on the windowsill instead of in the cleaning cupboard and thought I might be in trouble if Sister Eugenie spotted it.

Eventually I did go into a proper sleep. When I woke I felt woozy and all was quiet in the delivery room. Pale dawn light filtered through the curtains and I could see that the bed had been tidied up and there were screens round it. My tummy felt empty. I touched it. It was flabby and sore, and a large bandage covered the place that hurt. The baby had gone. Where was my baby? I was lost without that little person. I began to cry, as quietly as I could, so as not to disturb anybody. The nuns were already cross with me for being such a nuisance.

I couldn't see past the screens, but from across the room I heard a small snuffle and a sucking noise. The sounds filled me with hope. Carefully, because I was still woozy, I swung my legs onto the floor and tried to stand up. The stabbing pains where I'd been bandaged made me want to yelp out loud, but I was not giving up. Dropping onto my hands and knees, I managed to crawl past the screens towards the sounds. There was a big old dresser at the side of the room. The bottom drawer was open a few inches and the snuffling and sucking noises were coming from the darkness inside. Gently I pulled it open further and peered in.

There he was. I could tell straight away from his face that he was Curly's little boy, a long, strong-looking baby with dark hair under a white bonnet. He was lying on his back on a folded sheet in the drawer, wrapped tightly in a blanket. He'd managed to get one arm out and was putting his hand to his mouth, pulling and sucking at the cotton mitt. When I appeared he stopped and stared at my face. His eyes were still learning to focus and they were deep blue, like willow pattern china. I took off his mitten and he gripped my finger. The strength of life in him felt like a miracle.

Silver Cross Pram

1917

There was so much I wanted to teach him, and I knew with a heavy heart that we wouldn't have much time together.

I was in love with those willow pattern blue eyes, so like Curly's. I loved his long, exploring fingers, with nails like tiny crescent moons. I loved his smell, like gorse flowers. I loved the pale red mark under the soft hair on the nape of his neck. At first I thought it had been made when the doctor pulled him into the world for the first time, but Anna said it was a kind of birthmark called an angel's kiss.

Surprisingly, once he was born the nuns were kind to me, perhaps because they knew I didn't have long to enjoy being his mother. They called him Patrick, because he was born on St Patrick's Day, when March winds blew and buds were forming on the cherry trees in the convent garden. Curly would be proud for his son to have an Irish name, so I was proud too. Although I couldn't visit Curly because there was no privacy at the convent, I knew he was watching Patrick and me and was happy that we were safe.

Because the wound where I had been cut open needed time to heal, I wasn't given any heavy work in the laundry or cleaning floors. The nuns let me give Patrick his bottles and take him for walks in the walled garden. He sometimes made a fuss when he was left alone and I knew how to settle him. He loved me to hold him on the wooden seat under the cherry trees, where he could watch sunlight and shadows moving as the wind ruffled the blossom. At night I sang to him, mostly from Hymns Ancient and Modern. His favourites were 'All things bright and beautiful' and 'Eternal Father, Strong to Save'. I sang him 'Abide with Me' and told him what a special person his father was, good with animals and clever at making things, with a kind word and a helping hand for everyone. Once or twice, when I talked about Curly, it made me upset and this set Patrick off grizzling, so I couldn't stay upset for long. I would cheer him up by clapping my hands and making funny faces. He would stare for ages and do lopsided smiles if I made clicking noises with my tongue.

On the last day of April a brand new Silver Cross pram arrived for Patrick. I knew it must have cost hundreds of pounds because Olive had wanted one for Pearl, but Mr and Mrs Lyons couldn't afford it. The pram had shiny black body-work, with silver wheels and side trim, soft leather upholstery and a push-up hood to keep out the sun and rain. It was beau-tiful and I knew what it meant. Soon Patrick would be leaving with his new parents and I would never see him again.

'I'm going to run away and take him with me,' I told Anna.

'Don't be a fool,' she said. 'Where would you go?'

'I'll get a train to London,' I replied. 'I'll take his pram and sell it and we'll have enough money to rent a place.'

'The money won't last for ever.'

'Then I'll find work.'

'What will you do? You can't work with a small baby.'

'I'll take in washing and mending. Or make something to sell.'

Anna looked scornful. 'There's only one kind of work you'll make money from in London,' she said. 'And believe me, it isn't nice.'

I knew she was speaking the truth, because she had seen London and I hadn't. I'd never even been to the markets in Covent Garden where our family's tomatoes were sold.

'Look at that beautiful Silver Cross pram,' said Anna. 'Patrick will be well looked after and he'll be given things you could never afford to buy for him. Think about it.'

I thought about it. How could I provide for Patrick on my own in a big city?

'You'd only end up in some squalid lodging house with him,' she went on. 'You'd be too poor to feed him properly and he'd turn into a scruffy little tyke, running the streets with other scruffy tykes and getting up to all sorts.'

'But if I let him go he'll never know me,' I sobbed. 'He won't know he had a mother who loved him, or a father who would have been so proud to hold his hand.'

Anna thought for a moment. 'You can do as I did for Nina,' she said. 'Write him a note telling him who his mother is, so when he's old enough he can look for you.'

'The nuns would never allow that. Sister Annunciata told me we must never try to get in touch with our children once they've gone. It stops them from settling down with their new parents.'

'The nuns needn't know. There are ways of doing it...'

'What do you mean? Tell me how.'

'You have to do it secretly. You can hide a note for him where the nuns won't find it. Hide it in something your baby will take with him.'

'Did you do that, Anna?'

'Yes.' She looked round to check that no one was listening. 'I gave my daughter a locket, tucked in with her shawl. When you open it, it looks as though there's just a strand of baby hair inside. But underneath the hair is a secret compartment. I hid a photograph of me in there, with my name and date of birth. If she ever wants to trace me, she'll be able to.'

Anna was the cleverest person I'd ever met. I followed her advice. I didn't have a locket, but that evening I found a piece of paper in the chapel. I folded it like a card and drew a picture of Curly's carving on the front. Inside I wrote:

Patrick Searle, born in Hove, Sussex on March 17th, 1917. Much loved son of Violet Searle, born in Worthing, Sussex on September 9th, 1900, and Brendan Collins, born in Worthing, Sussex on June 8th, 1898, who died at the Battle of the Somme in July 1916. You are always in my heart, with love from Violet.'

I tucked the card behind the leather upholstery of Patrick's pram, under where he would rest his head. I was just in time. The next morning I looked out of an upstairs window. A smartly dressed older couple were wheeling the Silver Cross pram out of the convent gates, taking my son away to his new home.

PLEASURE GARDENS

1917

I couldn't think properly. All I wanted to do was find out where Patrick had gone. He couldn't be far away because the couple who took him had been wheeling his pram on foot. I was desperate to start searching for him, but confused about where to start.

Anna saw that I was in a dither and took charge. She told Sister Annunciata that I needed some fresh air and that she would take me for a walk and bring me back to the convent in time for evening prayers. To my surprise we were allowed out and given some small change to buy a glass of lemonade.

'Come!' Anna said firmly, taking my hand. 'There's a place I want to show you.'

We set off along a wide avenue with trees and posh mansions. After a few minutes we left the houses and passed through some gates. There was a big sign which said 'St Ann's Well Pleasure Gardens'. In my numb state it seemed to me that the place was magical.

'There's a hermit in a cave here,' said Anna. 'He's got a long beard but I think it might be stuck on. There's a monkey house. The monkeys are fun to watch. And there's a chalk well, which grew out of the ground from the tears of a lady.'

'A chalk well?'

'The soil here is chalky. Are you interested in geology?'

'Not really,' I confessed. I had no idea what geology was. I just felt sad for the lady.

'Good,' said Anna. 'Neither am I.'

We walked past cherry trees and showers of petals swirled across the path and into our hair. A blackbird was singing loudly from a bush with dark shiny leaves and big, deep red flowers. Behind it were more bushes with huge blossoms in pink, yellow and cream. I felt amazed, like I'd felt watching *Peter Pan* all those years ago, as if I'd stepped into a world of miracles where things happened differently from normal.

We could hear the sound of trickling water and followed it to a fountain in a lily pool where huge fish swam, as white as ghosts in the shadows, with flashes of gold from their scales. A few copper coins lay at the bottom of the pool. Anna said that people made wishes and threw them in. I wanted to pick one up to make a wish of my own, but she stopped me.

'It's bad luck to meddle with the coins,' she said. 'I have enough money for us both. Don't worry.'

There was an open grassy area with a little wooden booth. Outside it was a sign saying: *Hot air balloon rides. Book your tickets here.*

'Oh, Anna,' I cried. 'If only I could go up in a balloon, I might see the couple who took Patrick. I might see them walking him in the pram and find out where he lives.'

'The hot air balloon goes up only on Saturdays and it costs a fortune,' said Anna.

I must have looked crestfallen, because she added, 'Come. There's lots more to look at.'

We walked on towards a small tent. It was made of blue canvas, with golden stars stuck on and it had a sign outside saying: *Madame Tiger Lily. Fortunes told here.* A smaller notice at the entrance said: *No Entry. Reading in progress.*

'What book do they read?' I asked.

'Madame doesn't read from a book,' said Anna. 'She does Tarot card readings. People pick cards from a pack. She lays them out in special patterns and works out their meanings and then she gives advice to the people about their problems.'

That sounds really useful, I thought. I asked Anna if you needed to be very clever to understand it, and whether I could learn more about it.

'I'll tell you a secret,' she said. 'At weekends, when Madame gets lots of customers, I help her by serving people drinks in the queue and collecting the money. In exchange, she's taught me the patterns she uses and given me an old book about the meanings of the cards. I'm trying to learn them all. When I get my own Tarot pack I'll read your fortune if you like.'

'I would like that,' I said. 'You could tell me what to do next. You could help me find Patrick and bring him up properly, like a good mother.'

Anna smiled. 'The nuns don't approve of fortune telling, so you mustn't mention it to them. Mostly they turn a blind eye to what I get up to. Ivan, my baby's father, is giving the convent a lot of money so they are careful not to upset me. I still have to keep some secrets though.'

'They know you come to the Pleasure Gardens, don't they?' I asked. I felt lucky to be friends with someone like Anna, who seemed to make up her own rules. I could never get away with taking liberties the way she did.

'I've told them I come to the gardens as a volunteer in the glasshouse,' she replied, pointing to the top of a huge crystal palace behind the flowering trees. 'They think I'm learning to be a gardener.' She laughed. 'But there are no plants in the glasshouse. It's a film studio.'

I had felt knocked sideways by surprise so many times that afternoon that I suddenly went weak at the knees. Anna led me towards a building called The Pump House and bought us both lemonade with ice. We sat down at a table outside. The sunshine warmed us, the birds were singing loudly and she took a small metal flask from her bag and added a splash of clear liquid to each glass. What was it? It looked like water.

'It's a special Russian tonic,' she explained. 'Drink and you'll soon feel stronger.'

The tonic had a strange taste and soon I started to feel warm and emotional.

'Will you tell me some more about your life, please?' I asked. 'I've never met anyone from Moscow before.'

Anna thought for a moment. 'Shall I tell you about my little girl's father?' she asked.

I nodded, blinking hard to stop my eyes filling with tears.

IVAN

1917

The afternoon was getting stranger by the minute.

'You remember I told you my baby's father is also my mother's lover? His name is Ivan and he is a musician.'

I decided to look like a woman of the world and not show any shock, even though Anna's life was so different from mine.

'My mother knew him when she was living with her parents in Moscow. He was studying music at the conservatoire. He was very talented, but his family were poor. She adored him. They adored each other but my mother's parents forbade her to see him. They forced her to marry my father, who was a count and an officer in the cavalry. Ivan was broken hearted. He left Moscow and found work in London, playing piano for the Royal Opera Company.

'A couple of years later I was born. My father didn't like babies and never spent time at home. He left my mother for a rich widow, and my mother had to support us on her own. She taught herself to design and sew beautiful clothes. She has a good eye for colour and fashion and she made a living as a couturier for women in high society. After a few seasons she was offered work making costumes for the Ballets Russes. She knew Diaghilev and Nijinsky and we travelled to Paris with the company.

'By the time I was seventeen, there was a lot of unrest in

Russia. Poor people starved to death on the streets while the rich lived like royalty, dancing and drinking and feasting in their grand palaces. It was a hard, cruel time and we knew that soon there would be violence and revolution. When my mother was offered work in London, she decided to move away from Russia and to take me with her.'

By now the special tonic Anna had put in my lemonade had made me feel as if I was flying. In my mind I flew through dark city streets in Moscow, peeping through the windows of grand palaces where lights blazed, orchestras played and people in fine clothes danced and feasted. Then I was blown across a wild sea to London, to watch a room full of singers practising their songs while a man with sad eyes played music for them on a grand piano.

'And in London,' said Anna, 'we found Ivan. He was a composer by then, as well as playing the piano for films in cinemas, making it up as he went along. He had become quite famous and it was easy to find him. He has a house in Covent Garden and he invited us to stay while my mother was working round the corner. We never went back to Russia.'

'Does your mother still live with him?' I asked. I was trying to stay calm and act as if I had conversations like this every day. But how could Anna have slept with Ivan? How could her mother carry on living with a man who was unfaithful with her daughter?

Anna nodded. 'I can see you are shocked,' she said. 'But my mother forgives us. We all need to forgive and be forgiven, like the Lord's Prayer says. My mother says we were all responsible for what happened.'

Someone needed to tell Anna the truth. I couldn't stop

myself. 'But Ivan betrayed your mother. He's old enough to be your father. He should have known better.'

'It is easy to say that now,' said Anna. 'But we are human beings, not saints. Ivan looked after us both. We became like a family. My mother often worked long hours at night in the theatre and Ivan would take me out for a meal, or to watch him play the piano at a film. We loved going to this place called Late Joys. Performers and artists went there. I was proud to go with him. He is an attractive man and I loved to meet his friends who made films. One day I want to work in films and I was learning a lot.

'After a night out, Ivan and I would go home and have a glass of vodka and talk about everything under the sun. He said I reminded him of my mother when they were young in Moscow. He played me music he composed when he was in love with her. Tears would run down our faces. One thing led to another...'

She shrugged. Perhaps she felt guilty.

'Did you tell your mother?'

'After a few weeks of this, Ivan felt ashamed and told my mother. I did not have the courage. At first she was too upset to speak to me, but once she understood how it had happened she hugged me and said she loved me, but I must look for another place to live. Then I found out I was expecting and we all decided it would be impossible to keep the child. No one would be able to work with a baby around. My mother helped me find the orphanage, and Ivan's friend, Albert, owns the pleasure gardens. He makes films in the glasshouse and Ivan writes the music for them. Albert is moving to a bigger studio at Shoreham Beach and he's offered me work there making costumes and sets. It will be fun, working with lots of talented people and, guess what, Albert is going to make films in colour. Can you imagine?'

Anna seemed to know lots of clever and interesting people. For a moment I felt jealous of the way she seemed to take her luck for granted. I'd been disowned by my family and felt dull as ditch water.

A man with a monkey sitting on his shoulder strolled over to a barrel organ and turned the handle. It started to play 'It's a long way to Tipperary'. The monkey wore a red jacket with gold braid and a flat cap like a soldier's. He turned a coloured ball over and over in his tiny hands, squashing it and looking worried.

'Do you know how to sew?' asked Anna.

I nodded.

'Come and work with me on Shoreham Beach,' she said. 'Ivan has a friend with a bungalow there and we can share it. The job starts in two weeks.'

I felt myself go red with shame at my jealousy.

'Whatever you do,' she added, 'don't mention this to Sister Annunciata.'

ESCAPE

1917

Anna had the charm of a kitten with a ball of wool and the cunning of a farmyard fox. She worked out a way to get through the locked doors of the convent without needing Sister Annunciata's bunch of keys.

She won the trust of the nuns by acting as if she'd had a religious conversion, nipping into the chapel to attend mass whenever possible, kneeling to say prayers where she could be seen with her rosary beads, taking catechism classes and arranging the flowers for services. For bringing in flowers from the walled garden she was allowed to use the old wrought iron chapel key, kept high on an inside ledge. It could unlock the door to the outside at any time of day or night. Meanwhile, her afternoons were spent doing 'voluntary work' at the pleasure gardens, where she learned about the Tarot, helped in the film studio and made arrangements for the future.

Sometimes in the mornings we plotted together as we hoed the vegetable beds at the convent, but we had to be careful not to look suspicious by talking too often. The nuns must have thought we seemed an odd pair – Anna, so beautiful, bright and quick to learn, and me, plain, frumpy and slow. Every day I thanked Curly's angel for bringing us together and making it possible for us to be friends.

One morning in early May, Anna slipped me a note as we knelt together for prayers. It said: *Pack what you need and meet me in the chapel at dawn. Travel light.*

Although I didn't know exactly where we were going, I trusted her completely. I was afraid of looking suspicious if anyone saw me with my cardboard suitcase, but it was all I had to carry my nightdress, spare undies and little angel. They rattled around a bit, but I kept as quiet as I could so no one would hear us until we were out on the street, free as birds of the air.

Time dragged as I folded sheets that day and after dark I didn't sleep a wink, waiting for first light to show through the dormitory curtains. The girl in the bed next to mine woke with a cough as I sneaked out of bed. I put my finger to my lips and tiptoed across the floor, carrying my suitcase and shoes and trying to avoid creaky floorboards. Luckily I had a cardigan to wear over my thin frock. Although it was May the early morning was chilly and the grass would be soaked with dew.

I crept downstairs, along the passage and into the chapel by a side door. Grey daylight was starting to shine through the east window, with its stained glass picture of the Virgin Mary and baby Jesus. Out of respect I curtseyed to it and said a silent thank you to the nuns for their care. Then I prayed that Anna would come soon. Without her I was lost.

A few moments later she appeared in an Astrakhan coat, carrying a folded sheet and a small carpet bag. She took my hand and whispered, 'Courage, my friend!' It was the start of our adventure.

The big iron key for the outside door was on its secret ledge in the porch. Anna turned it in the lock and the door creaked open. We were out! Not completely free, but in the walled garden. The next bit was tricky. We had to climb an old apple tree, shuffle along a branch, tie a sheet to it and let ourselves down gently to the street on the other side of the garden wall. It didn't look dignified, but we managed.

'How do we get the sheet off the branch?' I hissed. It was dangling suspiciously over the street.

'We don't,' she said. 'We're not thieves so we'll leave it here for the nuns.'

She tossed the dangling end back over the wall and smiled. 'Look at us,' she said. 'We've escaped!'

I felt like shouting for joy, but she put her finger to her lips. 'Now to find Hove Station,' she said. 'We're catching the first train out.'

Luckily we didn't have much to carry, so walking was easy. We hurried past the pleasure gardens and turned left along a straight avenue of large terraced houses. A milkman driving a horse and cart trotted past on the other side, then to my horror we saw a drunk appear round a corner just in front of us. He was walking unsteadily, with red eyes, unshaven chin and whisky breath. The state of his coat was disgusting.

'Good morning, ladies,' he said, looking at Anna as if he'd found a gold sovereign in the gutter. He took off his hat, pretending to have airs and graces, and held out an arm. 'Shall we dance, sweetheart? Dance together until dawn!'

'Not today, thank you,' replied Anna. 'We're both off to see the doctor because we've got the clap.'

He stepped back in horror. Anna took my arm firmly and steered us both away. I could tell from the look on his face that the clap must be something really bad. Mother had told me that a woman should always be respectable and I believed she was right.

'What will people think of us if you say things like that?' I asked.

'Why should we care what people think?' she replied.

Why should we? I wasn't sure. Already that morning we had broken out of a convent, then disgraced ourselves in the eyes of a total stranger. But if nobody knew us, what did it matter? At that moment I hardly recognised myself.

As we waited on the station platform, clutching our tickets for Bungalow Town Halt, the sun appeared through early morning mist. We began to feel its warmth and the tracks shone silver as the train pulled in. Passengers got on and found seats: construction workers going to the Mystery Towers, labourers bound for the market gardens of Worthing, and the two of us, on our way to a new home on Shoreham Beach.

PANTOMIME ROW

1917

Travelling to Shoreham Beach from Hove, you have to cross the River Adur, which flows into the sea by the harbour. Curly had told me about the ferrymen, Fairy Page and Bully Bullock, who were friends of Uncle Mickey's and ran their boats out of Dolphin Hard. How exciting to arrive at our new place by boat! But on that morning in May our train carried us straight over the water and stopped by the farm road at Bungalow Town Halt. From there we walked along a shingly track.

I loved everything about the place. A skylark sang and sunlight bounced and sparkled across the water. Gulls swooped and dived into the waves and a cormorant sat on a wooden post, drying its wings in the salty breeze. Wild garlic had found places to grow amongst the pebbles, its white flowers spreading in streams like Lilies of the Valley. I wanted to pick some leaves for cooking with but Anna said to wait, because we didn't want our new home to stink of garlic.

We carried on down a dusty road known as Pantomime Row. There were lots of bungalows, all different. One looked like a castle and stood out. An important person must live there, I thought. Some were made from old railway carriages turned into rooms. We stopped at one called The Swallow. It was built from two railway carriages side by side on a flat concrete area, with a wooden roof across, so there was a room in between them and a porch in front. One of the carriages had been made into two bedrooms and the other into a kitchen and washing area. The room in the middle was a parlour and dining room. All the furniture we needed was there – beds with sheets, pillows and blankets, a sideboard with crockery and cutlery, a primus stove for cooking, and a silver candelabra full of candles for light. There were even curtains and pictures.

'Can we really stay here?' I asked Anna.

'Of course,' she said, tidying her hair in the mirror above the sideboard. 'This place belongs to Will, a pal of Ivan's from Covent Garden. His grandfather owns Late Joys. Will comes down here whenever he wants a break from London and he's bought several bungalows for friends and family to stay in. He's letting Ivan rent this one for next to nothing. It's more comfortable for us than Studio Rest.'

Studio Rest, I found out later, was where most of the film crowd stayed while they were working. It was the biggest bungalow, with about twenty bedrooms for cast and crew. The other bungalows were lived in by all sorts of people who had discovered they loved the place and made homes there. Mostly our neighbours were music hall and theatre people, and there were wrestlers and boxers, a jockey, surgeons, a barrister and a headmaster, all living side by side. Everything you needed was there. If it wasn't, someone would invent it. We soon found out about the places and people nearby.

There was Beach Green for sports and games, the Church of the Good Shepherd with its vicar who forgot things, a school for little ones, a horse-drawn cart bringing milk from the dairy, a grocer's for provisions, and a butcher's boy delivering meat on his bicycle. Mr Christian, the postman, sold stamps and collected and delivered letters. Old Joe, the night soil man, came round every evening to empty the buckets from our outside privies into his horse-drawn tank.

In summer there was so much to do. We could swim in the sea, go to the funfair, stroll to Dorothy's Café, play cards, have a game of cricket or take out boats with the rowing club. We often walked along the beach to enjoy the sea air, but we had to beware of Methylated Maggie, dressed in black, who had decided she owned the bit between two groynes and chased anyone who trod on her patch. If she caught you, you got whacked by her umbrella.

The film studio was a glasshouse with no electricity but the light reflected off the sea was so bright it was perfect in summer. Summers were for making films. It was the best thing. The camera crew used big mirrors inside the glasshouse to reflect sunlight on to the actors. When they could, they filmed scenes outside. They had to keep stopping to wind up the cameras by hand. When you looked into the viewfinder everything was upside down. I don't know how they managed to make the films come out right. They must have been geniuses.

There was one film they made called *Rogues of the Turf*, about a racehorse being stolen and taken out to sea on a barge. Ned, the horse, was brought to the studio by someone who looked like Uncle Mickey. I'd only seen Mickey once in Brandy Land and he didn't recognise me at the studio. I'd changed so much since the old days that I was hardly the same person. If he'd said 'How do you do?' to me I wouldn't have known what to reply, so I kept quiet.

The horse was gentle and well behaved about getting on the

barge, but I could tell he was nervous about being towed out to sea by a tug. The camera crew were hiding under hatches on the barge so they could film him without being seen themselves. Things got worse when there was a storm and the rope that attached the tug to the barge snapped. Poor Ned didn't like being adrift. He galloped round the deck a few times then jumped into the waves and swam back to shore. We tried to catch him but he'd had enough of the film studio and ran up Shoreham High Street, scattering passers-by. Luckily, Walter, one of the projectionists, was good with animals and managed to get hold of him and feed him carrots to calm him down. The camera crew on the barge were wet and seasick but luckily they managed to film Ned swimming and it all fitted into the story.

In another scene, Ned was in some stables and was supposed to get drugged by baddies so he couldn't run in a race. There was a vet with some chloroform ready to send him off to sleep, but Ned didn't like that idea. He kicked the chloroform bottle over and the vet and an electrician passed out on the stable floor with the fumes. In my mind Ned was as much a film star as Sybil Thorndike and Lady Tree.

The directors liked using animals and I liked helping with them. Once I was leading a goat into the studio for a scene in *The Mayor of Casterbridge*. It saw itself in one of the big mirrors used for lighting and went barmy. It pulled its lead rope out of my hands and butted its reflection. Splinters of glass flew all over. Some of the actors were very upset, because it's supposed to bring bad luck if a mirror breaks while you're filming. The glass was a nuisance to clear up, but nothing bad happened, not until years later.

In winter, scripts got written and props and scenery were

made and stored in the joiners' shop, ready for the next season. Winters were times to keep warm, to make costumes and help paint backcloths. We had fun doing other things, too. There were shilling hops in the church hall, and our friends Walter and Dougal used to take it in turns to dance with Anna and me. Anna seemed to like Walter and I didn't want to stand in her way, so I sometimes said I was tired and sat out with Dougal. He had red hair and his father was a gamekeeper on the royal estate at Balmoral. He knitted his own socks and gloves and made me a warm winter scarf in a Fair Isle pattern. I was grateful for it as on chilly days the winds whipping off the sea could give you a nasty nip. Dougal was very sensitive and never once made a pass at me. I think he knew my heart belonged to Curly and that's why he never tried it on.

At Christmas, we used to go to the Church of the Good Shepherd. There would be carols sung by the children, with candles in jam jars, and a harmonium pushed from place to place on a trolley with pram wheels. Dougal used to cook them treacle toffees.

Winter storms could be wild and frightening. One night, after we'd lived at The Swallow for a few years, a huge cargo ship was washed up near the old fort at the end of the beach near the harbour. The shingle under some of the bungalows got washed away. Luckily for us, ours was safe. If only Curly had been alive, he and I could have set up home so happily together on Shoreham Beach.

MOON

1918

Looking back, I probably got the gift of hearing voices around the same time I started my funny turns, but at the time I didn't think anything of it.

When I found the skeleton key and spoke to Curly on the other side, I realised I knew how to do things other people didn't. What I had always thought was just common sense turned out to be quite uncommon. It wasn't foretelling the future. It was more like being able to hear what people were thinking. How did I do it? Just by noticing the ways people moved, watching faces and listening for signals, like a dog does. I knew how to disappear into the shadows or the patterns of wallpaper. Being in service at the vicarage had taught me how to blend in with my surroundings, to clear my mind and be silent. That was part of the gift. Anna saw I had a gift and showed me my very own Tarot card.

After a few months at the film studio Anna had become the wardrobe mistress, but in the winter months, when there wasn't enough daylight for filming, she gave Tarot readings. She called herself Madame Magenta, the Voice of Verity, and dressed like a Russian gypsy. This was sensible as the fur hat and shawls kept off some chilly sea winds. She read the cards in a beach hut near our bungalow and I was her assistant. It was my job to collect money from customers and brew hot toddies on the primus stove.

In a quiet moment Anna read my cards and I got the Moon. The Moon was number eighteen in the major arcana. On the card was a picture of a lobster crawling out of some water up a path towards beautiful snowy mountains. I felt like that lobster. I'd made myself a shell so I didn't drown in sorrow when I lost Curly and Patrick, I'd clawed my way out of trouble at the convent and now I was on a journey to discover new places. Also in the picture were two towers, like the two lighthouses of Shoreham, where we were living. Then there was a dog and a wolf.

'Listen carefully,' said Anna. 'The dog represents our public and friendly face, and the wolf our hidden instincts, and they are two sides of the same animal. Do you understand?'

I nodded, wanting to learn more. Things Anna said about the meaning of the card helped me understand myself better. As a child I'd been taught to keep nasty feelings hidden and put on a friendly face, like a dog wanting to be loved. But in dark days, when the war changed everything and I lost Curly and Patrick, bad feelings took over and I'd secretly hated myself. I'd believed what my mother and Olive had said about me, that I was a disgrace to the family and no one would love me. When I told Anna about it, she said that understanding our own dark days could help us to know our own shadow side.

'If you understand your own shadow side,' she said, 'you needn't be ashamed of it or keep it secret. On your card the Moon looks down on the scene and is a guiding light, but she has her own shadow side. Shadows make everyday things look strange, so people feel confused and frightened by them. Someone like you, with a real gift, can help other people not to be afraid of shadows, to give them hope for the future. We could work together.'

I began to love the Moon. She was more than a Tarot card. She was part of me.

MEDIUM

1929

One night in 1922 a terrible thing happened. We were about to go to bed and Anna was having her usual glass of port when we heard a shout of 'Fire!'

'Don't worry. They're just trying out a scene for the next film,' said Anna, wrapping a shawl round her shoulders more tightly.

We really didn't want to go outside, as the night air was chilly. Then the shout came again, louder and more urgently. We grabbed our shoes and coats, opened the front door and looked out. The air was thick with smoke and we could hear the crackle of burning timbers.

Flames were shooting out of the windows of one of the bungalows, across the street and along from ours. Others nearby were catching alight. Stanley and Arthur Mumford, who owned the studio, were running around in their pyjamas, trying to organise a rescue operation. Arthur carried an elderly lady from her home and called us over to help haul furniture out of the nearby buildings onto the shingle. Walter and Dougal were bringing out cups of tea.

'What's happening?' Anna asked Walter.

'The Shoreham fire engine has been called,' he said, 'but it can't get here because the old bridge is being pulled down. So they've got to wait for the Worthing engine.'

By the time the Worthing engine arrived, the damage had been done. Luckily no one was badly hurt, but some people lost their homes and a lot of furniture floated out to sea on the morning tide. Our skin and clothes were covered in black ash from all the burning wood and paper and our hair smelled of tar. Everyone was exhausted.

Although the main studio was saved, with only a bit of damage to the glass, the Mumfords couldn't afford to replace all the equipment. Another company took over and made two films with an American actress called Florence Turner. She was beautiful and we all loved her because she never put on airs and graces, but after a few years the second company ran out of money too. In 1929 the studio closed down. It was such a shame, everyone losing their jobs. It was like losing a family. The film crowd moved on to find work elsewhere, mostly in London, and the bungalows were filled by holidaymakers.

Anna and I were lucky because our bungalow hadn't been touched by the fire, so we still had a roof over our heads. Madame Magenta's Tarot cards were a good earner, but once the studio closed we needed another income. Anna reminded me I had a spiritual gift and suggested we try a few séances. Contacting the other side was popular at the time because so many people had lost loved ones in the war and wanted to be in touch with them. Séances seemed a good way for us to branch out, especially with the holidaymakers.

To start with I didn't like the idea. I didn't want to trick people into thinking they were in touch with loved ones on the other side. I'd heard about fake mediums with hidden helpers moving things around in the dark and I didn't want to be involved with any jiggery-pokery.

'We've got to make a living somehow,' said Anna. 'We don't need to be fakes. You've definitely got a gift. A psychic person has a responsibility to help others, like a nurse helps patients to get better.'

I couldn't argue with that, so we started work.

Anna could make anything with scissors and a needle. She still had piles of silks and velvets and other marvellous materials the studio had used for making costumes and props. Soon our parlour was furnished like an Arabian tent, draped in emerald, turquoise and purple satins, trimmed with golden brocades and tassels rescued from *Little Dorrit*. The polished mahogany table was lit by our candelabra. The flames were cut into a hundred dancing lights by the crystal chandelier from *A Lowland Cinderella*. The effect was like snow falling softly, and the chandelier made a tinkling sound. It gave me a feeling like when I was small and watched *Peter Pan*. It turned the room into a place where you could find a way through to another world.

Still, the idea of going into a trance in a room full of people terrified me.

When I told Anna she just shrugged and said, 'It's what actors do all the time.'

'But I'm not acting. I'm being real.'

She looked at me and sighed. 'When you are being a medium,' she explained, 'you're going to call yourself Wendy Moon, aren't you? That's what we decided.'

'Yes, but…'

'Is Wendy Moon your real name?'

No, but…'

'Wendy Moon is who you are when you put on your costume

and perform for people.'

I felt uneasy. Wendy was Curly's special name for me and I wasn't sure about sharing it with other people.

'Wendy Moon,' Anna went on, 'is the person inside you who can give us messages from the other side.' She found a lovely primrose yellow shawl that shone with silver threads and wrapped it round my shoulders. 'When you put on this shawl you are Wendy Moon, a medium. When you take it off again' – she gently removed it and put it in the sideboard drawer – 'Wendy Moon goes to sleep until the next séance, and my friend Violet comes back. See?'

'When I lived in London,' she went on, 'Ivan took me to see a medium who went into a trance and gave the audience messages from the other side. People came from miles away to hear her. Before she went into a trance she moved her hands like a magician saying abracadabra. She did it again when she came back to normal. It was like a signal, like opening and closing the door to the other world. The audience understood straight away.'

I could see what Anna was getting at. I was still Violet underneath. But what was exciting was that I could also make myself into Wendy, who could fly out of her body and see and hear in special ways. It felt exciting and risky, having the power to do that.

'You need some props, like actors have,' said Anna. 'Let me think. There's a character called Moon in a Shakespeare play,' she said. 'Moon has a lantern and a dog. There's a lantern we can use from *The Mayor of Casterbridge*. I can put a beeswax candle in it and it will smell holy, like in church. The audience will think of spiritual things.'

'Next door have got a pug,' I suggested. 'They might lend him to us for a few evenings.'

'I'm not sure that would work. He's always scratching and snuffling and licking his parts. It might spoil the atmosphere.'

She was right. We needed a sound that was magical and would cover up any accidental rumbles of the stomach and such. We thought for a moment. Then suddenly I was inspired by a memory from long ago.

'Tinkerbell!' I shouted. 'You can be like Tinkerbell, with a light and a jingling bell, and lead me to the other world. The bell is the call to fly away and find the Lost Boys and everyone!'

Anna understood my idea at once. She said jingling the bell would be a perfect signal for me to become Wendy and fly away, then to come back again when it was time.

'Perfect!' she said. 'Now let's find some costumes in the pile I saved from the film studio'.

Because it would be dark in the séances we looked for clothes with silver and gold threads that would catch the light from the candles. For Anna we found a long silky black dress that shone when she carried the lantern near her face, but kept her dark when she used the bells and candle for Tinkerbell. Wendy's dress was pale blue satin and I tried it on with a lacy pinafore and tied up my long fair hair in two plaits around my head. It made me look young, like I looked when I was in service and used to talk to Curly by the garden gate. We agreed that when I was ready to fly I would wrap the pale yellow shawl around my shoulders and stretch out my arms for a moment like a bird, like Wendy waiting to take off from the window sill of the Darlings' house.

The bell would ring and I would feel the warm glow of

Tinkerbell's light. In my heart I would reach out to Curly, and through the dark of my flight I would search for the entrance to the other world. I had found it many times when I flew, and seen the skeleton of the winter ash key, silver in the moonlight. That was my key to the other side.

MAGIC LANTERN

1929

A nna made some posters to advertise our séances. They said: *Experience the wonderful world of Wendy Moon, spiritualist and visionary. Sign up for an introductory event to be held at The Swallow at 7.00 p.m. on October 28th. Entry by donation.*

The idea of séances gave me goose bumps of dread. I needed a serious talk with Curly. I found a quiet place on the beach, well away from Methylated Maggie. Then I used my gift to get in touch with the other side. Sitting comfortably with my back against a wooden groyne, I cleared my mind, took nine deep breaths of sea air and watched the little angel between my palms. The grain of her wood began to twist with energy and her face came alive. Then her wing tips began to shimmer. The whisper of the waves carried me upwards on the sea breeze. I shifted my balance and flew inland up the valley till I saw a sparkle of light around the ash tree. There was the magic key. I held out a finger and touched it, and I felt Curly's arms around me. It was wonderful.

For a while we floated together in the blue, like swimmers, eyes closed, holding hands. I knew he didn't want me to see his face, but I could feel his arms warm against mine and smell his lovely smell, like mown grass. He kissed my forehead. I kissed his hands.

'Lovely girl,' he said.

'Curly,' I said. 'I need your help. I've bitten off more than I can chew. Anna says I'm a spiritualist and visionary and people are coming in a few days to book tickets for a séance. They'll all expect me to get in touch with their loved ones and I don't know how.'

There was silence. Then he said. 'Tricky.'

'I should never have agreed to it. I don't want to be a fake. I hate myself.'

'You're not a fake. You've got a gift.'

'Yes, but it only works with you. I can't call up other people to order. What if someone asks for a message from their dead Aunt Mabel? Even if Mabel appeared, how could I be sure it was her? What if she said something nasty or rude or very personal?'

'Yes. It could be tricky.'

'Or if someone asked about a soldier who was killed, like you, Curly. It wouldn't be right to upset them.'

Silence again, then, 'What do you think, Wendy? It's you doing it, not me.'

'I don't want to upset people. I want everyone to go away happy.'

'Yes.'

'I want to give them hope for the future.'

'Yes.'

'I want to show them life could be better. Like in the theatre when Tinkerbell's light was fading away and everyone clapped because they believed in fairies and it saved her. It wasn't real but we all felt we could make a difference.'

'What are you trying to tell me, Wendy?'

'I suppose … I want us all to live in peace. If everyone believes it's possible we can make a difference. We could have been together now, you and me and little Patrick, if it wasn't for the war. Oh, Curly, I wish we could live here together on Shoreham Beach, like we planned.'

'I know, Wendy. But we can't be together because of the war. Let's hope there's not going to be another one.'

'I could tell people that in the séances but they might not listen.'

'I think you could show people. They'll understand better if you show them. Look at where you live, Wendy. You're next to a film studio.'

'It's closed down.'

'Aren't there still useful things about?'

I thought for a moment. 'Yes, there are. Anna knows where to find useful things. We can make up a story that will give the message to people. We could call it an evening of storytelling, not a séance.'

Curly knew me so well. I loved him for showing me what to do.

Anna found what we needed from the studio. She was still friendly with film people, especially Walter, the projectionist, who used to show the rushes to the directors after a day's shooting. Since the studio had closed down he'd found some work lighting shows at the Theatre Royal in Brighton, but he still lived with Dougal in a bungalow a few doors along from ours.

Walter knew how to work a wonderful machine called a magic lantern. It was a metal box, with a place in the middle for an oil lamp. On the front was a big lens, with space for two painted glass slides to fit behind it. You could move them around with a metal handle. The lamp light shone through them and the pictures were projected on to a wall. When you turned the handle it could look as if the pictures were moving. They looked best when the air was full of drifting smoke, so we lit some church incense and the atmosphere was really mysterious.

Walter painted some coloured slides to go in the magic lantern and showed Anna how to work it. It was up to me to do the voices for the people in the pictures. Dougal agreed to help with some music on his wind-up gramophone. Anna would start by introducing me as Wendy Moon and explain that the story they were about to see was transmitted to me by my spirit guide on the other side. She would light the lamp in the magic lantern, then ring the bell which was the signal for me to go into a kind of trance and do all the voices for the story. We made up a story about war, which reminded me of Patrick. Here is how we showed it. I will describe it like a scenario, which means a running order for scenes in a film.

In the first scene a happy couple are getting married in church, with 'Here Comes the Bride' playing on the gramophone. They say to each other, 'I will love you for ever.' Then there is a slide of 'Your Country Needs You', and the young man, now a soldier, gets on a boat which is tossed on big waves in a dark blue sea. Next you see a battlefield lit up by a full moon, with huge guns and a twisted tree that has lost its leaves. The young soldier and his friend smoke cigarettes together in a trench.

Next there is a deep rumble from the guns, which is made by Dougal shaking a metal thunder board. You see a weary horse nuzzling his dead master, the young soldier. 'I Vow to Thee my Country' plays on the gramophone. Then back to the poor twisted tree, which now has a white cross on either side of it.

Red poppies have grown in the muddy field. The young English soldier floats up above one of the crosses, and a German soldier floats up from the other cross. 'Hello Fritz!' 'Hello Tommy!' They wave to one another and fly away together through an evening sky.

Now the story goes back to England where you see the young wife from the beginning of the story. She is with a little boy. The boy asks, 'Mummy, will my daddy come home soon?' The mother replies, 'Your daddy died for his country, my darling. He can never come home.' The boy says, 'Are there other boys and girls who will never see their daddies?' 'Yes, my son,' says the mother. 'There are millions of children whose fathers went to war and will never come home.' 'Then war is wrong, Mummy.' says the little boy. 'We must never allow there to be another war.' Sad music plays. I am not sure what, but I think it is by Elgar, with a cello. I say, 'Grant us peace.' Anna blows out the lamp in the magic lantern and the story is over.

People seemed to love our evening shows and some came back several times. Even the vicar said he liked the story. The donations box filled up quickly. I wanted to give all the money to the Quakers, who believe in peace, but Anna was in charge and kept some. We had port to drink on dark chilly evenings, and took bus trips to the theatre in Brighton with Walter and Dougal. It made a change, which Anna seemed to need. Once most of the film people had left she began to get restless, wanting the fun of a big town and a chance of romance.

THE ONION PALACE

1930

Years later, when Anna was getting tired of Shoreham Beach, she announced she had found us a place to live near the Onion Palace in the middle of Brighton.

'I love that building,' she said. 'It reminds me of Moscow. I have found us both some work at the Royal Albion Hotel, on the sea front. It is very grand, very beautiful, with connections to the royal family. There are gardens nearby to walk in and a fountain with dolphins.'

'Real dolphins?'

'No, silly, real ones would die in a fountain. It is the Victoria fountain, with metal dolphins. You will love it.'

'Will we have to dress up in the hotel, Anna?' I asked. 'I don't think I've got the right clothes.'

'No need to worry. You will have a uniform. Walter has found us a place to rent in Gardner Street,' she replied. 'We'll have a room each. It's above a dairy and close to everything we need – shops, a market, theatres, pubs, and work at the hotel.'

'Anna, you're so clever! How did Walter find it?'

'He has a room there for when he's working late at the theatre. The other people he's been renting it with are moving out. We'll share a kitchen and the outside privy with him. Don't worry. He's quite fastidious in his habits.'

'Do you and Walter like each other, Anna?'

'Yes, of course. He's a good friend.'

'Are you courting? Is that why we're moving to the same house?'

Anna looked confused for a moment then she laughed. 'Oh my goodness! You mean you don't know? Walter is in love with Dougal.'

'But they're both men!'

'Yes they are. And they are very discreet about their love, because it is not allowed between two men and they could be arrested by the police. So you mustn't talk about it to other people.'

It took me a few moments to take this in. I decided to change the subject.

'What work will we do in the hotel?'

'I'll be a silver service waitress, because I have experience. The customers are rich and very particular. They like things just so. You can start in the kitchens, washing up.'

'Will we still do the magic lantern shows?'

'There won't be room for that in the Gardner Street place. Anyway, we could both do with a change. You could try putting up a sign for *Wendy Moon, Clairvoyant*. You could see clients by appointment in your spare time.'

I was excited about moving to Brighton. In the August when I was two, King Edward VII was crowned and our family went to Brighton for the celebrations at the Onion Palace. I was too young to remember it, but Olive was six and she told me lots of stories about it.

It was a hot day and we all dressed in our Sunday best and rode along the sea front in an open topped bus, as far as the Palace Pier. We didn't go on the pier because our parents believed that the pier attracted the wrong sort of people. There was a slot machine called What the Butler Saw, where you could put a penny in and see pictures of ladies in frilly underwear, or sometimes with no clothes on at all, running around a room called a *boudoir*. Olive told me that the pictures were rude and nice people did not look at that sort of thing, but so I could imagine what it was like she made up a game. I had to pretend to be a grown up lady with bare bosoms and she would be a man and chase me. If she caught me she would pinch my nipples and say, 'Ooh la la!' I had to say, 'Non, non, non' straight away or else she would hold me down and bounce around on top of me. Sometimes Frank tried to join in but we felt a bit shy playing that game with a boy.

Olive told me that on King Edward VII's celebration day our family shared a stick of Brighton rock. It was pink outside and white inside, with blue writing running all the way through it. Father cut it into pieces and Mother was cross with him for giving some to me, because I got pink sticky dribble all down my best frock.

The Onion Palace had a beautiful dome and minarets (Olive taught me that word), all lit up for the celebrations. Lines of coloured lights ran along the pillars and arches, as though the fairy folk had decorated them fit for a king. The gardens in front were full of Japanese lanterns in ruby, turquoise, amber and emerald. So beautiful did it look that our parents bought a framed print as a souvenir, and hung it above the sideboard in the parlour as a family treasure. Underneath the picture were the words: 'The Royal Palace, Brighton, drawn & pub, by J. Rouse.'

I loved to gaze into that old-fashioned world. On the skyline was the palace itself, like a vision from a faraway kingdom, standing proudly behind a wall and gardens with trees. A splendid carriage was driving by, pulled by magnificent bay horses, while people in fine clothes rode behind or stood watching in admiration. I used to imagine being one of the people in the carriage, on my way for a drive by the sea and a wonderful picnic, with crystal glasses and plenty of lemonade. When I grew up I wanted to be successful like them, living in a fine house with not a care in the world.

Although I was excited about moving to Brighton, it began to dawn on me that life was about to change in a big way. Anna had been restless for a while but I'd become attached to Shoreham Beach. It was the place where Curly and I had dreamed about making a home together. I might feel lost in a big town.

When I talked about it with Curly he said he would still look after me, wherever I was. If I felt lonely or afraid, I should remember my parents' picture of the Onion Palace, and how I used to dream of making a success of my life in the shadow of its walls. We'd made good with the magic lantern shows. Now it was time to move on and see what else Wendy Moon could do.

SUGARED ALMONDS

1931

I talked to Curly about the clairvoyant idea and he said, 'It's not really going to work in such a noisy spot, is it? Think about it.'

He was right. The sounds in my room would have made it impossible to concentrate on anything but the everyday world. From the crack of dawn there was a clatter of horses' hoofs and milk churns and a racket made by people working in the dairy, talking and laughing. The street itself was full of shops. You could buy anything from exotic cheeses to woolly socks, and Gardner Street ran between the station and the sea front, so trippers would pass by looking for swimsuits and buckets and spades. There were locksmiths and clock smiths and furniture makers and ironmongers and books and naughty postcards with drawings of ladies with big bosoms and men with eyes on stalks. At night there was music and loud chatter from the public houses. I didn't mind, but it wasn't the right atmosphere for a clairvoyant.

Walter suggested that I could try an advertisement in the *Evening Argus*. Readers could consult Wendy Moon by letter. People could send in their problems and questions to a box number, enclosing a postal order for one shilling. I could collect the letters from the *Argus* offices and reply to each reader's home address. This was a better idea than meeting in a noisy room. Walter even offered me the use of his typewriter, so my letters would look official. Anna taught me to type and to make carbon copies. Soon I began to pick up several letters a day. Anna helped and we shared the money.

One of the first letters to arrive gave us a shock. It said:

I am in a pickle. I have been courting an older gentleman and a few months ago he asked me to marry him. He said he would buy me a ring and I could help him choose one. I was delighted and let him become intimate with me. I regret this now as he no longer seems to care for me and becomes angry if I remind him about our engagement. Did I do wrong to give way to his desires? How can I win back his affections? Please help.

Yours faithfully,
L. Shinn (Miss)

Anna looked startled when she saw the name on the letter. All in a hurry she pulled last night's *Argus* out of the wastepaper basket and looked at the front page.

'Oh my goodness! I remembered the name. Laura Emily Shinn died a few days ago. She collapsed while she was out walking with her friend, W. Applegate Esquire, a hairdresser. The police are asking for anyone who knows anything about her to come forward.'

I went cold. 'What should I do, Anna?'

'You must take the letter to the police.'

'But she wrote it to me in private.'

'That doesn't matter now. She's dead. If you don't hand it over you're withholding evidence.'

'I've had enough of this. Anna. I don't want to be involved with this clairvoyant lark.'

'Don't worry, Violet. You're a good clairvoyant and you help lots of people with their problems. You've got a gift. Do you want me to take the letter to the police for you?'

'Oh yes, please Anna. You'll know what to say to them. I don't.'

I was unsettled by the whole business. It felt like snitching to me, going to the police, but Anna said it was important to tell the truth. She told me I was 'performing a public service' and made me feel better. Curly said it was the right thing to do.

It turned out that poor Miss Shinn had been poisoned with cyanide. Mr Applegate had told the police that she used it to dye her hair and it must have leaked into her food while it was in the same bag. The police were suspicious and called on Mr Applegate to say they were going to ask him more questions. After they left he got shot in the head and died in hospital.

Curly said it was obvious that he'd shot himself because he felt guilty about poisoning poor Miss Shinn. The police thanked Anna and me for handing over the letter and helping them in their enquiries. They said the services of a genuine clairvoyant could be useful to them in solving crimes. It made me nervous about opening any more 'problem' letters, but the money was useful. Anna could earn two pounds a week as a silver service waitress, but washers-up in the hotel kitchen only got half that amount and I wanted to pay my way. Most of the 'problems' were about love and marriage and just needed common sense.

Working in the Royal Albion suited us both. It was a short walk from Gardner Street and we had lovely food to eat as one of the perks of the job. Anna said that some of the customers gave themselves too many airs and graces, because they were in a hotel where the royal family and friends had stayed.

If customers were rude, some of the waiters got their own back by secretly spitting in their food. I thought it was disgusting but Anna laughed and said it served them right for being toffee-nosed. She was really friendly with a waiter who didn't think twice about spitting. He looked a bit Italian and everyone called him Mancini. He'd been around, spending a couple of years in the air force, boxing at a fairground, and playing football for Queens Park Rangers. He was light-fingered with the silver, nicking a few bits of cutlery at a time. Once he had enough to sell, he'd take it up to Whitechapel where he had a friend with a market stall. I didn't trust him, but after work he and Anna used to go drinking till the small hours with Violette, his 'missus' as he called her, and others. I wished her name wasn't so like mine.

I began to worry about Anna. She seemed to be under Mancini's spell. He was younger than her and spoke funny, but she started to copy his ways, smuggling bottles of vodka out of the hotel.

'Everyone does it,' she said when I pulled a face.

I didn't steal, except once when I filled my pockets with sugared almonds left over after a wedding reception at the hotel. When I got them home I noticed the almonds tasted bitter.

'Be careful!' Anna warned me. 'Some types of almonds can poison you with cyanide.'

I thought of poor Miss Shinn and threw away my stolen treats.

The Tunnel of Shadows

1934

If you travel by train to London from Brighton, you go past Preston Park, with its rock garden, waterfall and Chinese bridge, and then a few moments later you're underneath the Downs, in the darkness of Clayton Tunnel. Years ago, two trains crashed in the tunnel. Lots of passengers were killed and people say there are still lost souls trapped in the gloom. It's a soot black eerie place that made my throat grip tight and sent stabbing pains into my ears when we travelled through on our way to watch a show that Walter was working on at the Royal Albert Hall. The show was wonderful but I hated that tunnel and refused to do the journey again.

Anna didn't mind darkness. She said that growing up in Moscow had made her able to face most things. While she went on day trips to London I stayed behind and walked by the sea, or caught a bus to Rottingdean and had a picnic by the village duck pond. It was peaceful there. If it rained I always enjoyed spending time in the reference library at the Royal Pavilion, looking at books or reading the papers. I still thought of it as the Onion Palace and treasured my members' ticket. I loved finding out about local history.

I read about Brandy Land and how tomatoes were good for people because they contained lycopene, and baked beans in tomato sauce were not only tasty but healthy to eat. Although

I liked finding out about its history, I was never tempted to go back and visit Brandy Land. I wanted to remember my old home as it had been when Curly and I were growing up there, before all the changes.

Anna said I needed to leave the past behind and look ahead to the future. It was what she needed to do herself, but I knew we were different. We had been close friends on Shoreham Beach, but once we got to Brighton our differences showed themselves. It was a painful truth and one I learned in 1934, which I call the Year of the Tunnel of Shadows.

The shadows were imaginary and also real. Imagined ones came from my own sadness that Anna and I were no longer close like we used to be. I imagined her with her new friends – Mancini and Violette and her sister, staying out late into the night, drinking after work. Mancini had moved to a café on the seafront called The Skylark. Apparently he had a criminal record and kept moving jobs when it caught up with him. Walter told me he'd changed his name once or twice to avoid trouble. He had a scar on his upper lip as though he'd been in a fight, but it didn't stop him switching on the charm. He and Violette had parties at their place in Park Crescent, in a house that looked grand but was a bit grubby. Walter said their goings-on were 'seedy' and Violette used to entertain men who paid her for sexual favours. I couldn't understand how they could carry on like that together. Anna said if you took enough morphine you didn't care how you made your money.

I said, 'How does Mancini feel about her carrying on with other men?'

'I don't know. I'm not sure if he cares. They have terrible arguments, because she knows one day he will leave her.'

'Would you do what she does to get money, Anna, if you had some morphine?'

'Do me a favour, please. I'm not stupid.'

'I don't know what you see in Mancini,' I said.

She looked at me thoughtfully. 'No, I don't suppose you do. You can't see it because he's not your type. But when I'm with him I feel excited, as if anything could happen.'

I wanted to tell her, 'He's no good. He's a rotten apple and he'll make your life rotten too,' but I stopped myself. There was no point. Anna wouldn't listen. I hated Mancini then, for stealing my best friend.

'He'd better be good to you,' was all I said. She smiled and replied, 'He is.'

Then there were real shadows cast by two horrible murders. The first one didn't really have anything to do with us, but the second one did.

With the first murder, police found the headless body of a young woman in a trunk in the Left Luggage office at Brighton Station. Her legs and feet were found in another trunk, but there was no sign of her missing head. The police started a huge search to find out who she was. Hundreds of women were reported missing and staff were interviewed at all the hotels, including ours. It was horrifying to think there was a killer on the loose, who might strike at any time.

Mancini seemed particularly jumpy about the murder. Anna said that interviews with the police had made him nervous. He'd decided to move to Kemp Street, round the corner from us. Violette had gone to Paris for a holiday while he packed up and brought everything in a wheelbarrow to the new flat. His new rooms were nice enough, except for a whiffy smell, which Anna thought was a dead rat under the floorboards. A neighbour reported the smell and the police visited Mancini to investigate. It turned out to be coming from a trunk he'd brought over from Park Crescent.

Now comes the shocking part. Inside the trunk they found Violette's body, killed by a blow to the head. She wasn't in Paris after all. Had Violette lied to Mancini about going to Paris? Had he killed her and hidden her body? I felt completely out of my depth and terrified for Anna.

'He's tried to get rid of her,' Curly told me. 'I've never trusted that man. Stay well away from him.'

'Anna,' I warned her, 'you might be in danger. What if he's a murderer? He's lied to the police.'

But Anna was sure Mancini was innocent.

'It's true he's been hiding her body,' she told me. 'He told me he found her dead on the bedroom floor at Park Crescent. She must have been battered to death by a client. It's been a terrible time for him. He couldn't tell the police because he has a criminal record and he knew they wouldn't trust him. And he didn't want to bring shame on her by telling them about her clients.'

She started to sob. 'Now the police will put him on trial for a murder he never committed. It's so unfair. If they find him guilty he will be punished for someone else's crime. They could even hang him!'

I'd never seen her in such a state. Suddenly she took hold of my arms and pulled me towards her so hard it hurt. I stepped back but she clung to me and wouldn't let me go. Her eyes were wild.

'Violet!' she cried. 'You must help him.'

'I hardly know him,' I replied. 'How can I help someone I don't know?'

'Then do it for me. Help me,' she replied. 'The police trust you because you helped them before. Tell them you know he is a good man, an innocent man.'

She thought for a moment. 'You must say this. Say Violette came to you for advice, as a clairvoyant. She told you in confidence that she was seeing someone else, a bookie, because she was afraid she might lose Mancini and she wanted to make him jealous. It's true. She was seeing a bookie ... going out with a bookie and then...' Anna was thinking out loud. 'Yes. She became afraid of the new man, because he could be violent. She was worried he might harm her and wished she could go back to Mancini. She came to ask you whether she should go back to Mancini. She wished she'd never tried to make Mancini jealous.'

'And what was I supposed to say to her?' I asked.

'Say you told her to break up with the bookie and go back to Mancini because he's a good man.'

How could I tell them he was good? He was obviously a crook.

'Please, Violet. Please. Help me. Help him. He's innocent. I know he is.'

My throat tightened as if we were going through the Tunnel of Shadows.

Interference

1934

Curly warned me not to get involved.

'Anna's a lost cause,' he said. 'She fancies Mancini and can't see the truth any more. He's a liar and she's fallen for his charms. She thinks she's clever but he'll drag her into the gutter. You'll see. Walk away while you can.'

'She's my best friend, Curly. I've got to help her. She says Mancini's innocent. The police are putting the wrong man on trial. She loves him and they just want to start a new life together.'

'Don't be a fool, Wendy. It won't help her.' He was almost pleading. 'Don't tell lies for Mancini. You'll regret it for ever.'

'I owe it to Anna, Curly. Look how she helped me get through the dark days. If it wasn't for her I'd still be scrubbing floors in the convent. I'd never have had all those happy years on Shoreham Beach. I was there nearly half my life. It was where you and I dreamed of living together.'

There was a long pause. Then Curly said, 'I see you've made up your mind. But you'll be sorry, Wendy. Some people can lie and it's like water off a duck's back. But lies always backfire. You have to cover them up with secrets and more lies until you don't know what's real any more. You'll end up with nothing but shadows. You're throwing away your gift.'

That was how our conversation ended. For weeks afterwards Curly refused to speak to me.

The police were still interviewing hotel staff about the first body in a trunk. Two constables took me into a room at the Royal Albion, sniffing out clues. There were enough dodgy affairs among the hotel guests to keep the police occupied round the clock, but as the owner was a friend of the Prince of Wales, no one interfered. I said I had some information about Mancini. The older constable remembered me giving useful evidence before in the cyanide case and the younger constable eagerly scribbled down everything I said.

Anna had told me what the police already knew. Mancini had confessed to them that he'd found Violette's dead body at Park Crescent, hidden it in a trunk and moved it to Kemp Street on a wheelbarrow. He'd planned to keep it there, but the smell and leaking body fluids gave away his secret. He hadn't dared say anything when he first found her, because he had a criminal record and the police would think he'd murdered her. It was true that he and Violette had argued a lot lately, because she'd been seeing someone else.

This is where I made up some evidence. I said that Violette knew I was a clairvoyant and had come to see me for advice. She'd suspected Mancini of being unfaithful to her and wanted to make him jealous, so she'd started going out with a bookie. Quite soon she'd realised that her new man had a nasty temper and she wanted Mancini back. Although they sometimes argued, Mancini was always kind to her. I told the police that I didn't think he was violent. I said it was more likely that her bookie had lost his temper and hit her on the head in a fit of jealous rage when she told him she wanted to leave him. It was a lie and I hated myself the moment I said it, but Anna was counting on me.

It was horrible. During the interview I went into a kind of trance while I made up the lies. Anna had taught me how to keep my voice steady and act a part during those Evenings with Wendy Moon. I knew I'd lost her and it felt as painful as swallowing a large stone. But she'd been my only friend when I needed her and I wanted to repay her for looking after me.

Other friends were ready to give Mancini a good name. At his trial, friends testified to his good character. He spoke up convincingly for himself and it took the jury a couple of hours to come to their verdict: innocent.

Anna was overjoyed. Mancini declared that he wanted to leave the past behind. It had been a miserable affair with Violette, but now he and Anna were going to start a new life together in a flat by the Elephant and Castle. He was going to use his real name, which was John Notyre. Everything would be above board.

They found work together in a restaurant with a good class of clientele and moved up to London a couple of days later. I was at work when Anna left so we never said goodbye, but she left me a card to say thank you for helping to make sure justice was done. She said she had never been happier and I must come and visit soon. She forgot to enclose their address, but in any case she knew I would never visit. I never wanted to go through the Tunnel of Shadows again.

Walter had to move too. The Theatre Royal was having a difficult time with competition from 'talkie' cinemas. It had to close down for a while and he found more work in London. He was clever with lighting effects and easily found work. I missed his friendship and his funny stories about the films and shows he'd worked on. After he left I couldn't afford to stay in the flat on my own and didn't want to share with strangers. It felt like the end of an era.

It was impossible to get close to Curly, like trying to tune a wireless with a lot of interference. When I reached for the ash key to find him and talk about where to go next, he refused to speak. Eventually he told me I'd betrayed my gift by lying to help a criminal go free. If I knew it all, he said, why was I asking for his advice? I'd go my own sweet way.

'Serves you right if you're not happy,' he said.

I thought he was being stuck-up, like Olive used to be when we were children. I left him to stew in his own juice and tried to think what Anna would do in my place. She always had a plan.

Yes, of course. She'd go to the reference library. They had a good selection of newspapers. I could look in the advertisements for a live-in domestic job. I'd done that kind of work at the vicarage and I could find somewhere similar to live a simple life with no interference from the outside world.

Without Curly I'd lost my inner guide and felt I was just going through the motions of living. If there had been a way to find Patrick I would have searched for him, but I had nothing to start from. The nuns had given his new parents the birth certificate and forbidden me to try and look for him. He would be a young man now, with his own life. He'd been a clever baby. I knew that from his alert blue eyes. Perhaps he would be a student doctor or an engineer. I would never have been a good enough mother to help him find a career like that. The best I could hope for was that Curly would forgive me and he and I could be friends again.

MOONSTONE

1934

Among the jobs advertised in the *Evening Argus* was one for a live-in kitchen assistant at the French Convalescent Home near Black Rock. It was in a good spot – quiet, but just a short walk along the sea front to the Onion Palace. The nurses were nuns from Chartres, who spoke French and seemed very kind. The manager at the Royal Albion Hotel gave me a good reference. I'd always worked hard in the kitchens there, day and night, and I'd never taken time off, even during the troubles with Mancini. Sister Angela interviewed me at the French Convalescent Home, and she must have liked me because I got the job.

Once I started work I was given my own room on the top floor with a comfortable bed, a chest of drawers and some pegs to hang up my uniform. It didn't have a sea view, but I could look out over the rooftops and let my imagination fly like the gulls. It was a funny old building – grand, like a French chateau, with turrets at each corner, a colonnade and gardens overlooking the sea. It looked foreign among the Regency terraces, as if it had uprooted itself and blown across the Channel from France, landing in Kemp Town.

It took me a while to understand what kind of place it was. It had been built by the French government and the patients were a mixture. Some were recovering from operations they'd had at the French hospital in London. Some were English soldiers who had been wounded in France during the war, and stayed on because they couldn't face going back to the outside world. Some had been rescued after the Battle of the Somme and brought back to England in hospital boats. I wished Curly could have been rescued and come to stay with the kind nuns. It would have reminded him of going to church when he was a boy and he could have got his strength back and recovered.

There were children too – half a dozen wild ragamuffins whose families were working for the French government in London. They lived alongside the other patients like family pets, running round the garden and up and down the corridors. If they came into the kitchens looking for treats, Oscar the chef would make them stand in a line and give out bits of fruit or warm pastry. If there was any cheek he would threaten them with a rolling pin and shoo them away. They used to scarper down the corridor calling out, 'Oscar, tra la la!'

'You've done well, finding that place,' said Curly.

He seemed to have forgiven me and even came back from the ash tree to my little room. Some of the patients had fought in France during the war so he felt he was among his own kind. The interference had gone and we could talk to one another again, thank goodness. I began to realise that he hadn't trusted Anna since she'd become friendly with Mancini. The tension of having someone so unpredictable around had put a strain on our relationship. But at the Convalescent Home life was peaceful and ordered. Everyone was polite. Mostly the conversation was in French and I began to learn some.

'Bonjour, Madame.' Good day, madam.

'Je m'appelle Violet Searle'. My name is Violet Searle.

'Oui, je suis seule'. Yes, I am on my own.

'Bon appetit, monsieur'. Enjoy your food, sir.

'Merci, Madame.' Thank you, madam.

It was a soft, gentle language.

'Now you're here you can make up for lying about Mancini,' said Curly.

'How do you mean?' I replied. 'What's done is done.'

'If you were Catholic, you'd go to confession,' he said.

'What good would that do?'

'You'd confess what you'd done to a priest. He would tell you what to do to make up for it.'

'What difference would that make?'

'You'd be forgiven and you'd feel better. You'd be able to move on.'

'So the priest would tell me to say prayers with a rosary. Or scrub corridors on my knees?'

'Perhaps. Or maybe he would tell you to be kind and help someone in need.'

I gave some thought to this.

'I take care to clean and cut the vegetables so the patients can chew them easily.'

'That's good. Do you ask the patients what they need?'

'Most of them speak French and I can't say much in French yet.'

'Some of them are English. The ones rescued from the Battle of the Somme are English.'

'Yes, Curly. I wish you could have been rescued from the Battle of the Somme.'

After a moment Curly said, 'Have you noticed poor Captain Ashplant? He's got terrible shell shock. He shuffles around in his pyjamas and his wife comes on the bus every day to visit him. You could help them.'

I knew straight away who Curly was talking about. Captain Ashplant and his wife must have been middle-aged but they looked much older. Before the war they had set up a shop in Upper Market Street and imported jewels from India, where the captain had lived as a child. Mrs Ashplant seemed a nervous lady. For their engagement her husband had given her an Indian moonstone, set in an expensive Art Deco ring. I had noticed it one day when I was giving her a cup of tea and she had proudly held out her mottled hand to show it to me.

'I'm so very proud of it,' she told me. 'Isn't it beautiful? I'm just telling my husband about a book I'm reading called *The Moonstone*. It's set in India, where my moonstone comes from. The stone has special powers and it gets stolen.'

'It's a lovely ring, madam,' I said. The story sounded familiar but I couldn't think why.

When visiting hours came to an end, Mrs Ashplant caught the bus home. The captain looked uneasy and I wondered if he had indigestion. He seemed to be muttering to himself about a 'curse' and 'stolen' and shaking his head, then he wandered out.

As I was clearing away the tea things I heard a snuffling noise like a hedgehog coming from the bushes just beyond the colonnade. Sister Marie heard it too.

'Alors! Qu'est-ce que c'est?' she said, looking surprised. 'Ah, Violet, my dear. Please will you go and find out what is making these snorts.'

'Certainly, sister,' I said and went to track down the noise.

Captain Ashplant was on his knees in the bushes, scraping the soil with his bare hands. His nails were full of chalk and earth.

'Oh dear, sir,' I said. 'It's Violet. You do seem to be in a pickle. Let me help you.'

He looked up tearfully and his hands trembled.

'It's no good, my girl. It's gone. It's lost for ever in the plantation.'

'What's gone, sir?' I asked. 'Let me help you stand up. Your pyjamas are getting quite grubby at the knees.'

'Hang my pyjamas! Who cares about pyjamas? It's gone.'

'Gone, sir?'

'Someone has taken the moonstone. My poor May! The moonstone has been stolen. It's our engagement ring. I must get it back for her.' He let out a pitiful groan.

'Oh, Captain, sir, please do get up. What will the gardeners think?'

I had to be firm with him about getting up as he was too heavy for me to lift on my own. Luckily I managed to pull him to his feet and brush the leaves off his hair and dressing gown. Sister Marie appeared, to help me take him inside.

'Le pauvre capitaine!' she said. 'I will give him some brandy to help him settle down.'

We took him to his bedroom and I went upstairs to mine for a moment to think. How could I help the captain? I needed some advice from Curly.

'*The Moonstone* was one of my mum's favourite stories,' Curly told me. 'Don't you remember? She used to tell us the story, sitting by the fire on winter evenings.'

All at once I remembered our excitement, listening to Mrs Collins. That's why the title had seemed familiar.

'The captain's confused,' said Curly. 'He thinks the story in the book is really happening. The moonstone in the story has a curse on it if it's stolen. The local people put it back where it belongs to get rid of the curse.'

'So the captain thinks his wife's moonstone is cursed. What can I do to help him?'

'Explain to the nuns why he's upset. They'll find someone to give the story a happy ending for him.'

Suddenly I felt useful again. Perhaps helping the captain would find me a happy ending too.

DOC

1938

'J'aime la pierre de lune.' I love the moonstone.

'Le capitaine est content.' The captain is contented.

'Sa femme est heureuse.' His wife is happy.

A priest visited the home to drive away evil spirits from the moonstone. He spoke some Latin words, sprinkled holy water and moved his hands over May's ring as if he were playing a harp. For a while the captain forgot his worries and seemed contented, but a few weeks later the anxiety came back and he started roaming the gardens, muttering distractedly. He had to take sedatives to stop him digging up the flowerbeds like a demented terrier. The sedatives made him drowsy and he would sit all day in a wheelchair, hardly able to do his embroidery or to speak to poor May when she came to visit. What was to be done?

A young lady known as 'Doc' had started visiting the convalescent home once a week with her donkeys, Patience and Merrylegs, offering the residents what she called 'animal therapy'. She was training to be a doctor and in a minute I'll tell you more about her.

To my surprise, the nuns asked her to help Captain Ashplant with his anxiety. I pushed his wheelchair to the chapel and May followed with Doc and the two donkeys. The moonstone ring was wrapped in a pale blue silk cloth and we each placed a candle around it, very quietly. Patience and Merrylegs stood still as statues. Doc lit the candles and said a prayer:

'May all unhappy thoughts about this lovely stone disappear like smoke from the candles.'

She dipped the ring in some holy water and dried it on the silk. Then she handed it to the captain and May held out her finger, so he could put it on for her. It was as if they were renewing their marriage vows in a simple and peaceful way. We all felt calm and I knew Curly was there with me, wishing it was us getting married too. It was as close as he and I ever got to a wedding. The captain stood up and took May's arm to walk back to the home. Patience walked alongside him, in case he needed support. We left the candles alight, watching over our hopes for the future.

Over the next few years, I helped Doc when she came with the donkeys and we got to know one another. She wouldn't tell me her real name, saying she hated it and didn't want to be that person any more. She was studying to be a doctor. Some of the time she stayed in London, at the London School of Medicine for Women. The rest of the time she lived in a farm cottage on the edge of the Downs with her friend Grace. The farm belonged to Grace's parents, who had a flock of Southdown sheep. Grace trained sheep dogs. She was quite well known for it because in 1932, when she was only fifteen, she'd won a national dog handling competition in Hyde Park.

Doc kept chickens and the two donkeys. She gave two dozen lovely black hens to the home to provide everyone with eggs and to look after, as part of the animal therapy she was interested in. She used to go on about a man called George Mottershead who had suffered shell shock in the war and had started a zoo where animals and people could mix, because being with animals helped those who'd suffered trauma to get better. Some of what she explained went straight over my head and some of it made complete sense.

The donkeys were very gentle. Patience pulled a cart and took some of the residents for trips round the garden or along Madeira Drive to the Palace Pier. Merrylegs trotted along behind. He was always saddled up later to take the children for rides.

'Those children need fresh air,' said Doc, 'and it does everyone good to see the donkeys.'

In looks she reminded me of how I used to be, with the same wavy straw-coloured hair and eyes as grey as herring gull feathers. But her manner was completely different from mine. She was full of confidence, with a mind as sharp as a knife.

'Have you always been clever?' I asked one day, as we were walking the donkey cart along the sea front next to the electric railway.

'I found out quite young that I'd have to use my brain if I wanted to get anywhere,' she said.

'Did you learn that at school?'

'I worked hard at school. I needed to because my brother Clive was the blue-eyed boy at home. He was the favourite, the one who was going to take over the family business and fortune. If I wanted an interesting life I knew I had to make my own luck.'

I'd never imagined you could make your own luck. 'How do you do that?' I asked.

She looked at me as though I was a bit simple.

'You don't really make your own luck, but you can decide

how you want your life to be and make it happen.'

'I see,' I said. I didn't really.

'I worked hard and passed the entrance exam for the Girls' High School,' Doc explained patiently. 'I loved the science lessons. The teacher encouraged me and helped me to believe in myself. She told me I could get into medical school if I wanted to. The training takes years but it's very interesting. Look how lucky I am. I can do something I love and bring the donkeys to the convalescent home as part of my studies.'

'What do you study when you come here?'

'I make graphs for the patients who spend time with the donkeys and see whether it helps them to recover. They might suffer from trauma, or senility, or lack of moral control like some of the children. After I've been here I make notes about improvements in their condition.'

'Will you write a book about it?'

'Perhaps, when I'm a fully qualified doctor and my work will be taken seriously.'

When I told Curly about Doc, he came over very knowing and smug.

'It was obvious you two would get on,' he said.

It took me a while to understand why. Years later I found out why and was amazed.

PEACE AND WAR

1944

The Convalescent Home was orderly and peaceful, with loving care at its heart. For the first time in years my life felt calm.

My funny turns had settled down, ever since I'd learned how to be Wendy Moon at will and go flying in my head. I could simply close my eyes and take off to find the magic ash key, which let me talk to Curly or slip quietly into places I wanted to explore.

Looking back, it's odd that the 1940s were such a good time for me, because our country had been dragged into the Second World War. When will people learn that war is wrong?

It seemed to creep up on us. One day Doc and I were walking patients along Madeira Drive with the donkeys, smiling as we passed games of bowls on the green and a cheering crowd round the Pierrot show. A week later, all the entertainments shut down and strange shrouded shapes appeared under the arches; we found out they were anti-aircraft guns, hidden away so they couldn't be seen by German fighter planes. The promenade got covered in barbed wire, there were mines out at sea, and we had to put up blackout curtains so we couldn't be spotted after dark in an air raid. Hearing the drone of Messerschmitts on their way to bomb London was frightening and heartbreaking.

The only consolation was a rumour that Hitler would never

destroy the Onion Palace. Apparently he'd earmarked it for his own private use when he'd won the war. At least that was one place that would be spared from the bombs. Sussex Square, the Undercliff Walk and the Pitch and Putt at Roedean were not so lucky.

Curly was devastated.

'After everything we showed people on your Wendy Moon evenings!' he said angrily. 'Look how they're ruining this lovely world. Why don't they ruddy well listen and see sense?'

I told Doc about my conversations with Curly. She was curious to know all about them.

'Do you physically hear his voice?'

'Yes. I can only hear him when everything else is quiet.'

'And then can you hear him as clear as you can hear me now?'

'If I shut my eyes and concentrate.'

'That's most extraordinary. Paracusia, I believe it's called. I must do some reading about it.'

When Doc was interested in something she could sound really posh. It was probably brought on by the school she'd been to.

Apart from the threat of fighter planes from across the channel, the war years were fairly dull. Some of the older residents didn't understand what was happening and carried on cheerfully with their routines. Now and then a new patient would arrive, but we were in a backwater. The military hospitals were elsewhere.

Rationing meant extra care with the food. We were grateful for the eggs from Doc's black hens. She gave us a couple of cockerels too, so we could have chicken stew as a Sunday treat. Oscar the chef organised a team of younger nuns and residents to dig up part of the lawn and plant vegetables. Dig for Victory! The motto kept us going and we took no notice of broken nails, blistered hands or sore backs and knees. The new beds were full of carrots, onions, potatoes, spinach, cabbage, peas, beans and lettuce. When I watered them and fed the hens it reminded me of my days in the vicarage garden.

Sometimes I thought about Patrick and wondered what he was doing. Had he ever found my note, hidden in the pram? How silly of me to think a baby would know it was from his mother. Babies can't read. Had someone else found it and destroyed it? He would be a young man in his twenties now, probably fighting for his country just like his dad. I worried about him, though Curly told me not to. Patrick would come home, he said. When I asked him how he knew, he said, 'I just know.'

Not wanting to rock the boat by asking too many questions, I concentrated on growing vegetables and hoped that the war would end. Eventually it did.

'Dieu soit beni.' God be praised.

STRANGER

1956

The Convalescent Home was quieter after the war and I missed some of the residents who had moved on, one way or another. With fewer patients to look after, I no longer felt as much use.

'You need a change of air,' said Curly. 'You've been working at the same place for over twenty years.'

'I do love it here,' I said.

'Just use your ears and you'll know when to move,' he told me.

I was curious. 'Why, Curly? Will I hear something about Patrick?'

'Just listen out. Something important is going to happen.'

'How will I know it's important?'

'It may not be what you expect. It may seem strange.'

'Etranger.' Stranger or foreigner.

Genevieve, a young French woman, was brought to the Convalescent Home recovering from polio. She had been working as an au pair for the Marsh family in Hove and had caught the terrible illness that was going round.

'Ah, comme c'est difficile! Madame Marsh has young children to look after,' Sister Angela told me. 'With Genevieve ill, it has become very difficult for Madame to manage. She needs someone to live with the family and help with cooking and cleaning. She says there is plenty of room to stay in the basement. Violet, would you be able to move in and help, just until Genevieve recovers? Now there are not so many patients here, Oscar can do the cooking on his own.'

Was this the Important Something that Curly had told me to look out for?

'Of course, Sister Angela,' I said. 'I can help the family straight away.'

And so it was that I stepped into Genevieve's shoes. She never returned to her job as an au pair and I found myself living in Adelaide Crescent, in a house just like the Darlings' house I'd dreamed of as a child.

'You've landed on your feet there,' said Curly.

He was right. It was wonderful. The family helped me feel at home. Cleaning the stairs kept me fit and most days I took the children to the beach or the gardens while their mother did the cooking. There were five of them, all very lively.

A new Peter Pan's playground had been built on the sea front. I was excited to see if it brought back childhood memories of my magical visit to the theatre. The children loved it, but to me it was a disappointment. There was a roundabout with plastic teacups and saucers, another with little plastic cars and some plastic horses on springs to bounce on. The pirates and Hook and the crocodile and even Peter and Wendy were plastic, with dead looking eyes. It had no magic at all.

The children could be little scamps if they were cooped up, so I took them out in all weathers to run off their naughtiness. Mrs Marsh was full of energy and ideas and kept us all on our toes. She had trained as a nurse, which was just as well because there were always grazed knees and cuts and bruises needing attention. One of the children, Clare, needed a godmother and when Mrs Marsh asked if I would step in I was proud to be trusted. I daren't tell her I wasn't a Catholic and no one questioned it.

Mr Marsh had a Clarks shoe shop and played golf on Sundays. He was tall and thin and often seemed to be in another world. His fingers were long and he played the piano by ear in a beautiful and sometimes sad way that made me think of losing Curly and Patrick and feeling hopeless and unloved. There was a grand piano in the front room and I often heard his music drifting down the stairs. He played Chopin preludes or songs from musicals like *Porgy and Bess*. Beethoven's *Moonlight Sonata* was my favourite. Mrs Marsh told me he would rather play professionally than run a shoe shop, but he didn't have the confidence. He never played church music and didn't like religion, but the rest of us went to services at the Church of the Sacred Heart every Sunday. I even took communion.

'I've haven't been baptised a Catholic,' I told Curly. 'Will I be sent to Hell for pretending?'

'Don't you worry,' he said. 'There's no such place as Hell, except what people make for themselves.'

'Thank heaven for that.'

A FLY IN THE OINTMENT

1960

'There's always a fly in the ointment,' was my father's favourite saying.

I never understood what he was talking about. Mother said he was a pessimist. He kept himself to himself and if I tried to ask him anything he'd say, 'Here comes Trouble!' or 'Oh no, it's Lizzie Dripping again.' When I'd lived in my dream house in Adelaide Crescent for a while, it dawned on me what he meant. Nothing is perfect; there's always a catch.

I had the basement to myself, except for the rooms full of clutter along the corridor at the back. Mrs Marsh told me she would sort these out when she had time. I had a bedroom in the front, a huge kitchen with a sink, a dresser, a table and chairs, a gas cooker, and a cast iron range for warmth, and a yard at the back where I kept Phyllis and Myrtle, the hens Doc had given me.

I shared a bathroom on the ground floor with two lodgers. The first, Brother McBurney, was a retired monk. He had once taken a vow of silence, but trouble with his nerves had meant he'd had to leave the order. He was still very quiet and considerate, a real gentleman.

The other person who shared our bathroom was the fly in the ointment, capable of ruining anything. His name was Major Briggs, but it might as well have been Major Disaster.

He was the loudest, most unpleasant person I've ever met and he fancied himself as a ladies' man, twirling and waxing a bristly handlebar moustache. In his room he had swords on the walls and a tiger skin rug. He boasted to anyone who would listen about how he had saved an entire village in India from the man-eater.

'The brute was terrorising the natives. Of course the local chaps were too cowardly to take action but I saved everyone by stalking it. Tracked it down to its forest lair and opened fire. Damn fine shot, straight through the heart. It was the first of my many conquests. Ha ha!'

It wasn't only dead tigers he boasted about. He used to drum on about his prowess as a polo player. He had a stack of back copies of *Horse and Hound* in his room, piled up next to the electric heater and used as a table for his whisky decanter and glasses.

'I always had an eye for a good horse. One can't always tell quality from the blood lines. Need an expert eye for confirmation, don't you know. Then of course it's the way you train them. Spare the whip and spoil the horse, I say.'

When Doc visited me with the donkey cart, he appeared at once at the front door with riding boots, spurs and swagger stick, seizing a chance to impress the ladies.

The donkey pulling the cart was Patience's son Horace, a strong brown fellow who could sum up a situation in seconds. Sight of the major instantly put him on his guard. He laid back his long ears and showed the whites of his eyes.

'Good morning, ladies!'

We were startled by the loud greeting and even more when the major exclaimed, 'This one's a vicious beast, by George!

One can see by the flaring of its nostrils.'

Horace took a step back and bared his teeth as a warning. The major brandished his stick and poked Horace in the ribs.

'Have to show the brute who's in charge,' he announced, with masculine authority.

'And what has that to do with you?' said Doc. 'Kindly leave my donkey alone.'

'You see, dear girl, this donkey needs to be taught a lesson. No good being soft with them. Take it from an expert.'

The major moved closer to Horace, taking hold of his bridle and giving him another prod with his stick. Horace was by now very cross. With a loud snort he stamped on his attacker's toe and nipped his fingers so that he had to let go of the bridle. The major let out a yelp, then shouted, 'Have at you, sir!' He lifted his stick ready to take revenge on Horace.

I couldn't stand any more of his cruelty and shouted, 'No you don't, you bully!'

Grabbing the stick I yanked it out of his puffy hand and snapped it in two. I felt a sharp stabbing pain in my wrist, but fury drove me on. I got hold of that stupid moustache, one end in each hand, and twisted for all I was worth. The major whimpered in pain but I carried on. Curly was at my side, cheering.

'Think of those poor dead tigers and all the horses he's whipped,' he whispered. 'Let's give him a dose of his own medicine.'

I picked up the stick from the gutter and poked the two roken ends into his ribs, again and again, as hard as I could. must have hurt because he whimpered.

'How do you like the feel of your stick?' I hissed. 'Don't you hurt an animal again, or you'll have me to deal with. And frankly, I'd be annoyed to see your ugly face anywhere near me. I'd prefer it if you keep out of my way.'

He turned and limped slowly back to his room.

'You've certainly made your point,' said Doc, when he'd disappeared. 'And so did Horace.' She scratched his ears and gave him a carrot.

Although I was confident I'd done the right thing in preventing cruelty to an animal, I was also shocked by my own viciousness.

'Have I gone too far?'

Doc was smiling. 'You were magnificent,' she said. 'The major will be alright once he gets over the sore ribs, which he thoroughly deserved.'

She looked at my wrist, which had swollen and was starting to throb.

'It's not broken,' she said, 'but it looks like a nasty sprain. I haven't got a first aid kit with me so I'll take you to your doctor's surgery to get it bandaged up and put in a sling.'

Although it had felt like the right thing to stand up to the major, I didn't want to lose control like that again. I confessed my fears to Brother McBurney.

'You could try a vow of silence for a while,' he suggested. 'Silence can be a great healer. It teaches us to think before we speak. So much of what we say nowadays is thoughtless and causes regret.'

He showed me how to take a vow of silence and to write in a notebook for people when I really needed to communicate. It was sometimes inconvenient not to speak, and I made exceptions for Curly and Doc, but it did make me think about what was really important to me. I decided to start writing down some of my memories. After all, I was sixty years old and it was time for me to retire, to draw my old-age pension and to pass on what I'd learned to the next generation. I wished I could find Patrick, but hope of that was fading. I'd given him up and I wasn't allowed to look for him. I hadn't been a fit mother. He would have to find me, which seemed impossible.

Meanwhile, the major asked to move to a room on the second floor, so we no longer needed to use the same bathroom. While he was carrying his things upstairs, he dropped a cannon ball and cracked the glass in the hall floor window that let light into the basement. A few weeks later, I started to notice more empty whisky bottles than usual in the dustbin, which was a worry. When I asked Curly for advice, he just said, 'Each to their own.'

A nice quiet couple, Mr and Mrs Smith, moved into the major's old quarters on the ground floor. They were respectable and polite and kept regular working hours. It was peaceful downstairs without all the bluster and boasting.

I went for daily walks along the seafront, wrote my memoirs and met Doc once a week for fish and chips at the Regency Restaurant. I did allow myself to speak to her, so I didn't lose my voice altogether. She was still writing about me as a 'case study' for auditory hallucinations and kept detailed records of what I told her about my talks with Curly.

'I do feel guilty about the major,' I said. 'He's been drinking a lot since our argument.'

Doc thought for a moment.

'Guilt can be useful for helping to maintain our moral compass,' she said. 'It's like a conscience, isn't it?'

I nodded.

'But sometimes people get paralysed by it and it stops them from taking any action. They get bogged down and that's not useful, is it?'

I shook my head.

'In case you ever need to talk about anything,' she added, 'I'll leave you my card. It's got my phone number at the hospital.'

'I've never used a phone. I don't know how.'

'Is there someone you trust who could help you?' she asked.

I trust Curly, I thought, but you can't ask a dead person to help you make a phone call. I put her card in my pocket without reading it and we forgot about telephones.

BROKEN CHORDS

1964

Days turned into weeks, then months and years. Not much happened, though there was a lot in the news about 'the space race' between the Soviet Union and America. They both seemed determined to crash their rockets on the moon, leaving ugly piles of metal over its beautiful surface. The piles of litter on the seafront were bad enough, without sending rubbish into outer space. Why couldn't people be grateful to live in the world we have, without wanting to conquer more and more? Next thing we knew the Americans would be leaving their flag on the moon.

Suddenly my routine was shattered by two unexpected events. The first happened at teatime on a chilly March evening. Someone shouted, 'Fire!' and I thought, this has happened before. I ran up to the ground floor and saw Mr Marsh hurrying outside with two of the older children, wrapped in blankets.

'Susie's in the bath,' he shouted to me. 'Go and get Susie'.

I didn't think twice and started running upstairs to the bathroom on the second floor. It was next to the major's room and the higher I climbed, there was more thick smoke in the air. It caught in my throat and made my eyes sting and overflow with tears. I had to pause for a moment so as not to have a coughing fit. I could hear seven-year-old Susie's voice calling

'Mummy' and starting to whimper. The bathroom door seemed to be locked.

'Susie!' I called. 'It's Violet. Open the door for me. Let's find Mummy.'

'No,' said Susie. 'It's all smoky out there. I want Mummy.'

I mustn't make her panic, I thought. What can I do?

'Come on, poppet,' I said. 'The donkey lady's coming.'

It was a lie, but it worked. Susie loved animals and straight away I heard the key turn in the lock. Thank goodness. Just in time. I wrapped her in a towel and carried her down the stairs. By the time we got outside there was an ambulance with blankets to keep her warm in the chilly night air. At that moment I felt like the sort of person who is a good mother, like a member of the family.

I found out later that the major had been out shooting rabbits and his boots had let in water. He'd hung his socks up to dry over the electric fire and settled down for a nap before tea. One of his socks must have dropped onto the glowing bars of the fire and caught alight. Flames flickered out to the pile of *Horse and Hound* magazines he used as a table and they began to smoulder. Luckily, one of the children spotted smoke curling out under his door and raised the alarm. Everyone acted quickly. Mrs Marsh wrapped the children in blankets and took them out to the gardens. Mr Smith rang the fire brigade. Mr Marsh made sure there was no one trapped in the upstairs rooms and tried to persuade the major to come outside before the stair carpet caught fire.

The major was determined to put out the blaze himself. His curtains and tiger skin rug were now engulfed in flames. He kept running to the bathroom to fill a child's bucket with water and throw it at the fire. Finally, his window frame caught fire and glass exploded out onto the street. At last he consented to be pushed and pulled outside to safety.

What a mess! The fire brigade arrived, fixed their hoses to a hydrant and doused the fire with jets of water. Flames were bursting out of the attic windows and lighting up the sky like distress flares. An ambulance arrived, though miraculously no one had been hurt. Newspaper photographers took pictures of the house and asked for names and stories about what had happened.

The upstairs rooms were blackened with smoke. Bits of charred curtain and cushion floated down the stairs in a waterfall of debris. The fire brigade managed to dampen everything down so quickly that, apart from broken windows and soggy plaster, there was hardly any visible damage. The basement was untouched by the flames. Curly must have looked after Phyllis, Myrtle and me. Mrs Marsh said that St Anthony watched over the household and kept us all safe. Perhaps she was right.

The second surprising event happened a few days later. Mrs Marsh was looking for spare bedding to replace what had been lost in the fire. She asked me if I would see if there was some in any of the lumber rooms down the back corridor. I was curious about what was behind those closed doors.

In the darkest corner of the end room, under a dust sheet, I could see the shape of an old-fashioned pram. Imagine my surprise when I removed the dust sheet and saw a Silver Cross pram. My heart gave a leap. It was black, just like the pram Patrick had been given at the convent. It had silver wheels and trim, just like Patrick's pram. And the cream leather upholstery was the same colour as the upholstery on Patrick's pram.

Memories came flooding back. I could see his little head resting on the pillow. I could see the angel's kiss birthmark just above his hairline. I could see myself writing the note to let him know he had loving parents. My heart started beating fast.

Carefully I felt underneath the mattress. There were some mouldy crumbs and a teething ring and ... it was there, the piece of paper with my faded message. Patrick had never found it. How could he have done? He'd only been a baby.

I was overcome with sadness. Tears ran down my face and I had to sit down unsteadily on a dusty packing case.

'Help me, Curly,' I said.

'You've had a shock,' said Curly. 'Don't try to rush anything. Breathe slowly. If I could hold you tight, I would.'

'Why do I fail at everything?' I asked him. 'I've got so close to Patrick and now I've lost him.'

'Steady on, Wendy. Some things are dark and mysterious. Remember the Moon. Remember you're not afraid of the shadow side. You can still find him. It'll be a shock to him too, facing up to secrets from the past. He's a grown man. He's getting on for fifty.'

'I don't understand, Curly,' I said. 'How can I find him? His pram's been left here, but he'll be gone by now. He's probably in a new house with a family of his own.'

'Yes,' said Curly. 'But he might have stayed. What if he's still here?'

'There's no one called Patrick here.'

'They might have changed his name, the people who adopted him.'

'Oh no, not the major. Please don't let him be the major.'

'No. Not the major. The major's older than you. Come on,

Wendy Moon. Fly out of your dark and secret place and find the light.'

Just be quiet and let Wendy Moon take over, I told myself. Don't speak. Just fly till you see the magic ash key. If you think you've found Patrick, how will you be able to tell if it's really him? What will you hear? What will you see?

Slowly, as I flew, the voices reminded me. They reminded me of music I'd already heard and of what I needed to see. They reminded me of secrets in the shadows, of feelings I'd never admitted to myself and of hope for finding my son.

Dr Edwin Harrison MD, Palmeira Practice
Notes on an initial interview with Miss Violet Searle,
which took place at her home at 10.30 a.m. on Tuesday
9th June 1964.

Miss Searle is a registered patient at the Palmeira
Practice, but has not visited the surgery since 1960,
when she needed treatment for a sprained wrist after
an altercation with a neighbour.

I am carrying out a clinical assessment of Miss
Searle's mental condition, following a phone call from
Mr Thomas Marsh, her landlord. He is concerned that
her behaviour has become erratic and that she may need
institutional care. During the week before my visit,
according to Mr Marsh, he was bending down to check
the electricity meter in her flat when she held him by
the scruff of his neck and started to examine the back
of his head in a 'frantic' manner. When he asked her
what she was doing she looked at him 'strangely', folded
her arms as though cradling a baby and started to hum
the tune of 'Abide with Me'. Mr Marsh reported that he
feared she was going to 'grab me and pin me down' and so
he 'fled back upstairs with the greatest possible speed.'

When I arrived at Miss Searle's flat, Mr Marsh had
informed her of my intended visit and she showed me
through to her basement kitchen, with what might be
described as a polite but grudging air. Both she and
the kitchen appeared clean and orderly, almost spartan
in appearance. I introduced myself and she handed me
a piece of paper to read, informing visitors that she

is an elective mute and would write down answers to any questions I wished to ask. This was helpful as her written replies constitute an accurate record of her responses to my queries.

To test her awareness of current affairs, I began by asking the standard questions about today's date and the name of our prime minister. She provided me with a copy of *The Telegraph* and wrote:

VS: You will find the answers to those questions here, Doctor.

Clearly she is able to reason and to avoid topics in which she has little interest. Next I needed evidence of long-term memory and asked her to describe the house where she spent her childhood.

VS: I lived in Brandy Land with my parents and my brother and sister. My parents grew tomatoes in glass-houses. I was the youngest. When my sister got married and started a family there was no room for me so I had to find another home.

Miss Searle seemed reluctant to offer further information on this topic, so I decided to test her short-term memory by asking what she had eaten for breakfast.

VS: Egg sandwiches.

EH: Is that your usual breakfast?

VS: Yes. I keep two hens in the yard so I have lots of eggs. I sometimes add cress, which I grow on a flannel on the window sill.

EH: Do you have a varied diet?

VS: Egg sandwiches are quite enough, thank you, Doctor.

Although Miss Searle seemed perfectly capable of providing for herself I was concerned about the monotony of her diet. I suggested she might like to eat different foods sometimes and could enjoy more variety if someone else cooked her meals.

VS: I prefer to cook for myself.

I asked Miss Searle whether she slept well. She nodded affirmatively.

For certain individuals living alone can lead to delusional thought patterns. I suggested that she might benefit from more frequent company.

VS: I prefer to live on my own. I have company when I need it.

EH: I am not sure that you have adequate company here, Miss Searle. You seem to be quite isolated. Mr Marsh feels uncomfortable about visiting you. If you were to be looked after...

VS: I will not go to an asylum. I know what you are thinking. Never put me in one of those places.

As Miss Searle had adopted a frank approach I decided to question her directly about the incident with Mr Marsh the previous week. I asked why she had tried to comb his hair.

VS: I thought I saw something on his head.

EH: He was upset by your behaviour.

VS: He is easily upset. He always has been.

EH: What made you think you had the right to comb his hair?

VS: It would take too long to write down.

EH: I need an explanation, Miss Searle.

VS: You think I am mad but I am not. Over the years I have been doing some writing about my life. I will let you read it so you will understand what is true.

EH: Thank you. That would be helpful.

VS: I need time to put the papers in order. Come back next week please, Doctor.

I informed Miss Searle that I would visit her again at the same time next week to collect the papers. I finished the initial interview and left at 11.15 a.m.

My initial observation of Miss Searle suggests that she is vulnerable, skilled at concealing problems and possibly subject to delusions or psychosis. From information supplied by Mr Marsh, the 'company' she mentions is likely to be a hallucination.

Her 'papers' should be useful in diagnosing her condition. If they suggest mental instability, I shall recommend that she is moved to the Sussex County Asylum at St Francis Hospital, Haywards Heath.

CODA

June 11th 1964

By now, Clare, you'll have put two and two together. You'll have worked out what I was looking for when your father came to check my electricity meter.

I must have been too emotional and frightened him when I searched under his hairline for the angel's kiss. I can't tell you what it meant to me when I found it. So many memories flooded back. I remembered rocking him to sleep and humming 'Abide with Me' to soothe him. He loved music, even as a baby. He would always stop crying and listen. I suppose I hoped if I hummed the tune he might remember who I was: his real mother. But by then he'd decided I was completely mad and I don't think he would have believed me if I'd told him the truth.

Why did it take me so long to realise who he was? I was in a secret place of shadows and never imagined that he could be my son and that I could have so many lovely grandchildren. Now I feel proud. Curly is so proud too. He would have loved to get to know you all and you would have loved him.

It was a shame that the doctor was brought in. Doc got me a copy of his notes on our meeting. He thinks I need care, but a lunatic asylum is definitely not a place where I'd feel at home, so I've made my own arrangements. By the time you find this, Doc will have come to collect me with Phyllis and Myrtle. We are going to stay in her cottage on the farm. As a thank you to your family for your hospitality we've left some speckled brown eggs on the kitchen table for you to enjoy. They are lovely to eat soft boiled with warm buttered toast.

If you ever want to get in touch, you can do it through Doc. She's a Consultant Psychiatrist at the Royal Sussex County Hospital, and here is another unexpected surprise: her name is Dr Pearl Lyons. She's my niece, your cousin.

When I first found out, I was amazed. So that's what Curly had meant when he knew Doc and I would get on well. My mouth opened and closed like a fish. I must have looked as funny as Pearl when she was a baby in the hospital. I began to think about both of us leaving our families and finding our way alone. We both found out what we were good at. We both invented different names for ourselves. Making up our own names helped us to feel free to be who we wanted. Do we understand each other so well because we are related to each other? Is it because we grew up in the same house? Perhaps, but Anna understood me and we were from different countries. She could see behind my friendly face and into my shadow side.

It doesn't really matter who your parents are. That's a kind of accident. What matters is what your heart tells you. I know your father can be kind and loving. I've heard it in his music, along with sorrow and darkness. Listen to your heart, Clare, and don't be afraid of shadows. Follow your own path and enjoy the adventures!

MOONLIGHT SONATA

Clare: June 28th 1964

How weird and amazing that Miss Searle is our grandmother! I gave her story to Dad and told him it was really important. Then I watched him read it. He read quickly as though he was gripped by it, looking pale and finding it hard to breathe. For a moment I thought he was going to say she was mad and she'd made the whole thing up, but he handed the story to Mum and asked her what she thought.

Mum said finding his mother was a miracle and we should light a candle for St Anthony. She said the angel's kiss is proof he's really her son. How could Miss Searle possibly know about his birthmark if she wasn't his mother? Mum told Dad to read the story out loud to us all. The little ones didn't understand it all but, after he'd read it out, I felt like you feel after a storm, when the rain has washed away a lot of dust and grime and you can see everything more clearly. I felt so proud that she was my godmother first and that she wrote to me because I can be trusted with something so important.

Now Dad seems to have lost a weight off his shoulders and we don't have to tread on eggshells, like before. Now he knows he was loved and wanted as a baby and it wasn't his fault he had to be given away. He really enjoys playing his grand piano and he's started entertaining people in hotels and restaurants in the evenings. It's what he's always wanted to do but never had the confidence. It makes lots of people happy, especially him. We go and watch him and feel so proud when people clap and call for more of their favourite music.

The family have made a plan. We've written to Doc and invited her and Miss Searle to the house for a special tea. Mum will bake a cake and Dad will play the *Moonlight Sonata*. Horace is invited too. Miss Searle doesn't have to speak if she doesn't want to but I'm guessing we'll be asking lots of questions. We've chosen the *Moonlight Sonata* as a celebration for Wendy Moon.

The sonata is in three parts and Dad says the music is like his mother's story – dreamy at the start like moonlight on water, then sad in the middle when she loses Curly and Patrick and feels she's done wrong, then towards the end she finds her own strength and lots of amazing things happen quickly.

I'm so excited about her visit. I used to be frightened of Miss Searle and her scary rooms in the basement, but not now we know who she is. We were all afraid of secrets that might come out about Dad's mother and why she gave him up. No more secrets. No more being afraid. We're going to celebrate finding our grandmother and the *Moonlight Sonata* will echo all around the house.

POSTSCRIPT

Names in Violet's story have been changed but the house in Adelaide Crescent, Hove, is real, as I remember it in the 1960s.

The story is dedicated to Isobel, my husband David's grand-mother, and her family. Her grandchildren – David, Jeanne, Madeleine, Brian, Christine, Anthony and John – grew up not knowing their true family name or the identity of their grand-parents. Tom and Movita, their parents, were both adopted as young children and neither of them knew their birth families. Movita, in particular, felt it was a painful subject that should be left alone. She had been christened Lilian, but had changed her name to Movita.

Tom discovered the identity of his mother, Isobel, shortly after she died. She had given birth to him as an unmarried teenager and had been sent to an asylum, where she remained until her death, sixty years later. Once there, she never spoke, though she played the piano. Perhaps her gift for music was passed on to Tom, who was a professional pianist in later life. He never found out the identity of his father.

Violet's early life has similarities to Isobel's. Both lived through two World Wars. Both had an older sister and a brother who died from tetanus, contracted while cutting tomato shoots. Both had a son they never knew. Both left home under a cloud, never to return.

Some of the characters in the story are invented and some are based on real people. Genevieve, the family's au pair girl, really did contract polio and stayed at the French Convalescent Home. Mancini, whose name turned out to be Tony English, finally confessed in 1976 to the murder of Violette Kaye, over forty years after her death. There genuinely was a major with a tiger skin rug who was a lodger and who accidentally set fire to the house. There was a retired monk, too, who became a family friend. The donkey girl was inspired by relatives who understand therapy and whose animals are like members of the family.

Some dates have been altered for the sake of the story. I apologise for inaccuracies. Background research has opened my eyes to fascinating local history. Amazingly, the pioneers of the film industry on Shoreham Beach were world leaders in creating narrative sequences and the use of close-up shots. George Albert Smith, who owned the pleasure gardens and glasshouse studio by St Ann's Well in Hove, invented Kinemacolor. The Mystery Towers were real, as was the cyanide poisoning of 1931. The incidents with the horse at sea and the vet who was accidentally sedated are based on fact. Places have been recreated in imaginary ways, using memories of countryside and streets I knew as a child.

The internet has been an invaluable source of information. One book in particular provided an entertaining and surprising read about the Shoreham Beach film industry. It was *Bungalow Town: Theatre & Film Colony* by Neb Wolters (1985).

A huge thank you to Ali, Annie, Vonny and Jane, writers and friends who helped develop initial ideas and tidy up loose ends. Without your encouragement and early inspiration, Violet's story would never have emerged. Thank you to my children for commenting on early drafts and to the publishing team at 2QT, especially Catherine for clear explanations, Mandy for eagle-eyed proofreading and Charlotte for inspired design.

Above all, thank you to David, who shared personal memories, family history and reflections, and put up with endless tapping at the keyboard while the story took shape.

ABOUT THE AUTHOR

Leonie Pearce was born in Sussex and lived in East Anglia and West Wales before moving to Yorkshire in 1986. She worked in a laundry, in cafes and restaurants, in the Bodleian Library, for the Royal Mail, in theatre and cinema box offices, as an artists' model and a teacher, before becoming a Senior Lecturer in Drama. The work took her into schools, devising theatre for children, always with a chance for audiences to participate. Performance projects included persuading the King of Winter to bring back the sun, staging a trial to determine whether Lady Macbeth was responsible for her actions, and being Dragon Detectives to help an absent-minded professor preserve habitats for magical creatures. She lives down a track in the Yorkshire Dales with her husband, David, close to their three grown up children and four grandchildren.